SAVING FACE

THE FACETAKERS BOOK 1

SAVING FACE

FRANK MORIN

Saving Face

Book 1 of The Facetakers

This is a work of fiction. All the characters and events portrayed in this book are fictional, and any resemblance to real people or incidents is purely coincidental.

ISBN: 978-0-9899005-2-2 Paperback edition

A Whipsaw Press Original

Cover art by Christian Bentulan
(https://coversbychristian.com/)

Book design by Kate Staker
(https://katestaker.com/)

First Whipsaw printing: 2013

OTHER WORKS BY FRANK MORIN

Find all books on www.frankmorin.org

THE PETRALIST SERIES

Set in Stone, Book One

A Stone's Throw, Book Two

No Stone Unturned, Book Three

Affinity for War, Book Four

The Queen's Quarry, Book Five

Blood of the Tallan, Book Six
(release in late 2020)

When Torcs Fly, A Petralist Origins novella:
Tomas and Cameron

Game of Garlands, A Petralist Origins novella: Anika

THE FACETAKERS SERIES

Saving Face, Book One

Memory Hunter, Book Two

Rune Warrior, Book Three

Aeon Champion, Book Four
(release in November 2020)

SHORT STORIES

"Odin's Eye," included in *A Game of Horns:
A Red Unicorn Anthology*

"The Essence," included in *Dragon Writers:
An Anthology*

"Only Logical," a purple unicorn story

"The Seventh Strike," included in
Cursed Collectibles: An Anthology

CHAPTER 1

With a rattle and a bang, the restraining gate dropped away and released four modified go-karts. Marilyn cheered as gravity dragged her kart down the ramp and onto the road in a smooth acceleration toward the first of many curves in the steep, winding two mile track.

Marilyn's young boyfriend Bill somehow managed to pull ahead, followed close behind by long-time friends, Walter and Gladys. The couple rode close together, laughing and looking spectacular. Walter's chiseled good looks and gymnast physique drew every eye not already glued to Gladys' beautiful oval face or her waist-length, silky black hair that blew behind her like a sable cape. They looked fantastic, as they should. Marilyn knew exactly how much they'd paid for those looks.

Marilyn grinned as she followed the others around the first turn in her kart that was little more than a seat on wheels with a plastic body, steering wheel, and brakes. Gravity did the work of the engine on the steep track, dragging them forward, faster and faster until they barreled down the slope at reckless speed.

Dense forest of oak and maple lined both sides of the mountain track, their summer foliage forming a vivid green corridor through which the group raced. The warm breeze against her skin felt delicious, and Marilyn grinned wider at the long-forgotten sensation. It felt great to be outdoors and active again.

In the second curve, Marilyn's kart skidded in some loose sand, sending a thrill of fear rippling through her. She hadn't done anything so wild since she was a foolish girl.

I'm acting like an old lady, she chided herself and forced the worries away. *I need to act my appearance, not my age.*

She spared a glance down at her recently acquired figure and drew confidence from its youthful strength. Described as 'The All-American Girl,' she had perfectly proportioned curves and light brown hair that fell in bouncy waves past her shoulders when not crushed down by the racing helmet.

The men pulled ahead and skidded around the third curve with loud whoops. Gladys tried to follow, but over-steered and nearly lost control. She braked hard and barely avoided plowing into the safety rail.

Marilyn took the curve more slowly and called out, "Are you all right?"

"Of course," Gladys laughed. "You worry too much. You know I can't get permanently damaged."

"Just don't die."

"You're such an old maid. Enjoy the youth you've been given."

"I wasn't *given* anything. This youth cost a fortune."

"So enjoy it!"

Gladys took the next curve without slowing. Marilyn followed close behind, repeating Gladys' words in her mind, trying to ignore the cautionary voice of experience telling her to slow down.

They raced another half mile that way, pushing the little karts as fast as they dared, skidding around corners and laughing until Marilyn's cheeks hurt. Fear and adrenaline coursed through her like she hadn't dared feel for decades.

Bill maintained a slender lead despite Walter's efforts to pass, and Marilyn smiled at the rivalry. Although only in his twenties, Bill reminded her so much of Charlie, god rest his soul, that she felt she'd known him far more than two months. He made her feel as young as she looked, and he'd begun hinting his interest in taking the relation-ship to a more intimate level.

The thought set her heart fluttering like a young maid, a feeling she never expected to experience again. Could she risk telling him the truth?

As they swept around the next long curve, they found the road ahead blocked by three karts clustered together near a fourth, overturned. Several teen-agers were kneeling around a companion who sat in the road holding a bloody head.

Walter and Bill stopped nearby and climbed out to help. Marilyn braked hard behind them, and her kart shuddered as it skidded to a stop.

Gladys didn't slow. She screamed as she bar-reled down on the group in the road, managed to swerve around them, but over-steered on the far side. Her kart skidded, slid sideways across the road, and struck the guardrail still moving way too fast. It rolled up and over the barrier and Gladys disappeared beyond the steep edge of the road, still strapped in to the wildly tumbling kart.

"Brakes failed," Walter said as he entered the hos-pital room where Marilyn sat watching the uncon-scious and heavily bandaged Gladys. "Police are interviewing the owners of the track."

"Did you hear from Alterego?"

"That's the only good news. They're going to transfer her to their facility later today."

"Does she have comprehensive coverage?"

"Yes, thank the lord. Full face value."

CHAPTER 2

lterego proved efficient as ever and Gladys returned home the very next day. As soon as Marilyn received word, she rushed over to the large, craftsman style home her friends had custom-built four decades earlier in the Maryland countryside.

Walter answered the door, and Marilyn stared at his altered features. "When did that happen?"

"Last night while I waited."

"Is this really a good time?"

"Come on back. She's by the pool. You'll see."

Marilyn followed him through the richly appointed home to the spacious back patio. Gladys lay on a padded pool chair, enjoying the summer sun in a swimsuit cut to accentuate her lovely new figure.

"Marilyn," Gladys said and rose to greet her. She stood at least four inches taller than she had the day before, with a full-bodied, voluptuous figure with thick blonde hair and long, perfectly shaped legs.

Marilyn stared. "That's not 'Athlete's Dream.' That's . . ."

"You got it," Gladys said with a grin, "'Every Man's Dream.' Number one rental this year."

"How did you get it? The wait list is forever."

Walter removed his shirt to better show off his new, heavily muscled body. "Like I said, full face value coverage. Insurance replacements trump new rentals. Every other top fifty model was already out. This one just came back in yesterday from a three month lease."

Gladys laughed, "I couldn't have planned it better." She ran a hand across Walter's bulging pecks. "When Walter found out what I was getting, he just had to upgrade too."

Marilyn smiled, "I'm so glad things worked out so well. You look fabulous."

"What about you?"

Marilyn glanced down at the young, beautiful body she'd grown to love over the past three months, and made her choice. She could not pass up this singular opportunity at a second chance at life.

"I'm going in today to tell them I want to keep it."

"Good luck, dear. You'll be the first."

CHAPTER 3

I hate feeling old," Sarah said as she moved her sagging, wrinkled old body through the pool in time with the water aerobics instructor.

"Just think about this month's bonus," Jill said from where she exercised close by in the warm pool.

"Is that really all you think about?"

Jill smiled, showing perfect white dentures. Today she was a short, wrinkled old lady with wispy gray hair, although her face didn't fit the shape of the head very well. "Why not? It's better than whining about how miserable it is exercising these old bones."

"I'd think you'd be furious," Sarah said as she started a set of lunges that pushed her aching frame to its limits.

"Why? The payout's going to be awesome."

"I'd still be ticked. Instead of enjoying a little home time, you're stuck exercising that old relic."

Jill shrugged. "It's what we do, remember? We're donors. Why are you so surprised when renters come knocking?"

"It's not that," Sarah said with a frown. "It's . . . I'm just frustrated that old biddy got rewarded with your body after wrecking poor Tawnya."

"She's a top ten renter. It's in the contract." Jill stopped and faced Sarah. "What's really bothering you?"

Sarah blew out an old lady smelling breath. "I'm just anxious. I get my body back today and I'm suddenly worried what this old crone," she jabbed a finger at herself, "has been doing to it."

Jill shrugged. "If she damages it, you get the insurance payout."

"I know. It's just, I miss being myself."

"Who you are doesn't depend on what you look like," Jill said with a smile, quoting the poster hanging over the door in the cafeteria.

Sarah splashed her and focused on pushing the old body through the exercise routine, but her mind wasn't in it. Since voicing her concerns, she realized she'd been feeling that way more and more over the past few weeks.

Something needed to change.

CHAPTER 4

While they showered and dressed after class, Jill pulled a magazine out of her locker and tossed it onto the bench beside Sarah. "Check it out." She pointed to a cherry red sports car whose name was a mix of numbers and letters. "That's my new baby."

"Another one?"

Jill lifted the magazine and kissed the hot car with her wrinkled old lips. "Oh yeah. With this latest bonus, I can get a pre-production model."

"Why? You never drive the other ones."

"I know, but this one is the hottest new model. My collection is worthless without it."

Sarah toweled her hair, careful not to dislodge the wig. "You'll never buy out your contract if you keep blowing your bonuses."

"Why would I want to do that? There's no other job in the whole world like this one. Can you see me getting a normal job?"

"Fat chance. You're the number one rated donor. You'd have rich guys lined up to ask you out."

Jill shrugged. "They'd get rid of me as soon as they saw next year's top model, just like they did Irina."

"That's completely different, unless you decide to go nuts."

"Doesn't matter. Once I moved into her spot and she dropped out of the top ten, it's like she fell off the face of the earth."

"Still, it's worth a try at least, isn't it?"

"I don't see why." Jill looked genuinely puzzled. "I've got it easy here. Why change things?"

They made their slow way down the plush carpeted halls of Alterego's corporate facility toward the Corporal Transfer Lab where they would turn in the old bodies. They entered their normal transfer station, a plain white hospital-like room complete with beeping equipment, antiseptic smell, and four standard hospital gurneys.

The two beds in the center were empty while the beds to either side held the bodies they would inhabit after the transfer. A shiver tickled Sarah's spine at the sight of the waiting bodies, their heads and necks encased in sterile life-support units. The shining aluminum boxes with their rounded edges, beeping lights, and opaque faceplates always made her a little uncomfortable.

So instead she focused on the rest of the body, clearly visible beneath the thin sheet. It looked like she'd been assigned the same young body she'd worn for the past week. The consistency helped. She didn't like trying on too many different models. Every new one only made her miss her own that much more.

Not Jill. She loved the jumps.

"Hello, ladies," Tomas said with a grin. He motioned them toward the beds and helped first Jill and then Sarah lie down.

He was not a young man, but not old either. Sarah had asked him his age a couple of times, but he always deflected the question, usually with a joke about how her own age changed so much it didn't really matter. Wearing the old crone, she wouldn't give him the chance to tease her again.

He lingered beside her as she settled onto the gurney, watching her with his serious brown eyes. "And how are you doing today, Miss Sarah?"

"The mind is willing . . ." Jill quipped from her bed.

"But the body has arthritis," Sarah finished.

Tomas smiled. "Well, soon it won't be your problem any more."

He was a rather plain looking man, but he always looked her in the eye, and sometimes she felt she could see his solid, dependable soul. He'd grown

on her over the past months until she looked forward to his teasing.

While he busied himself preparing the injec-
tions, she asked Jill, "Don't you ever get tired of
other people using your body all the time? Don't
you want it back?"

Jill shrugged. "They keep it in good shape. I
get paid a lot. I can do what I want and don't have
any responsibilities."

"You're hopeless."

The growing feeling of discontent sharpened
into a resolution in Sarah's heart. When she had
first signed up as a donor, dazzled by the incredible
salary and potential for fame, she'd felt much like
Jill. Over the past couple of years, even as she broke
into the top ten and her pay skyrocketed to obscene
levels, she found herself less and less content with
the situation.

"When I get my body back tomorrow, I'm done."

"What do you mean?"

"I'm taking the early out option."

Jill gaped. "That'll cost a fortune!"

"I don't care. I don't want to do this any more.
I just want to be myself."

"Are you crazy? You'll kill your career." Jill rolled
up onto one elbow. "You're number five. A couple
more years and you'll be so rich you'll never have to
work again."

"It's not worth it." The truth of her words seemed so obvious she couldn't believe Jill didn't agree. "I'm leaving. I'll just take the jet down to the Caymans and spend some time in my beach cottage."

Jill frowned. "You don't have a beach cottage in the Caymans."

Sarah frowned in turn. Of course she didn't. Why did she just say that? For a second, she'd been convinced that she not only owned that cottage, but recalled vivid memories of visiting there with her family.

She didn't have a family.

Sarah managed a weak laugh. "Just kidding."

"Don't worry about it. These old ladies are rubbing off on us." Jill jabbed her sagging flesh. "Just the other day, I caught myself shopping for birthday cards for my grandkids! How weird is that?"

"I'll take the house in the Cayman's," Sarah replied. Jill's comment disturbed her more than she wanted to admit. One more reason to get out. The technology was so new, she didn't doubt there were risks the company had never revealed. After tomorrow, she'd be gone and wouldn't have to worry about inhabiting creaky old bones again until they were hers, decades in the future.

"You wish," Jill said as she settled back onto the bed.

"Maybe I will take a vacation down to the Caymans. Wouldn't that be great?"

"Sounds good to me," Tomas said, breaking into the conversation. "Want some company?"

Sarah started to smile. He'd been hinting in recent weeks that he was interested, and now that she'd decided to leave, she was suddenly tempted to take him up on the offer. But when she met his gaze, her smile faded.

His normal open expression was missing. He looked preoccupied, as if he'd made the offer because it was expected, as if he was playing a part.

From her gurney, Jill said with a wicked little grin, "Maybe Tomas should upgrade you to a sexy little number and the two of you can sneak away somewhere private."

Sarah would normally have blushed, but Tomas' odd behavior had rattled her and the jibe didn't dig like it should. She glanced at Tomas to see how he reacted. He smiled at Jill, but his expression darkened momentarily.

In the next instant his normal, open smile returned. The change came so fast if Sarah hadn't been watching, she never would have noticed.

Tomas said, "Or maybe I'll find a pretty little model for you, Jill."

Jill laughed. "You can't play me, Tomas. I know you're just hoping to get me alone when my own body gets back."

Sarah forced herself to smile along with the others, but she wondered at Tomas' sudden change. Despite Jill's number one rating, he'd always paid more attention to Sarah. Why the change? Why now of all days?

Tomas moved to Jill's side, slid a needle smoothly into her arm and injected the pre-transfer tranquilizer. "See you on the other side."

"Can't wait . . ." Jill's voice faded away as the fast acting drug knocked her out.

Tomas moved to Sarah and prepared the second needle. He met her gaze for a moment, and he looked troubled. As the needle slid into her arm, an odd chill shivered down Sarah's spine.

Must be the drug.

CHAPTER 5

T he next day, Sarah could barely contain her growing excitement as she headed for the transfer lab after lunch. She walked as fast as the old body she wore would allow. The renter would be pleased. Sarah had improved the body's strength and overall health during the rental period through the company's carefully designed exercise and nutrition program. Hopefully the old lady had returned the favor.

Sarah pushed through the door into the transfer station, unable to suppress a grin as she scanned the room for the renter and her precious body. The smile faded to a frown. Instead of the renter a tall, dark-haired man she recognized as Alterego's head lawyer waited in the room. He dressed in an expensive suit and carried a black leather briefcase.

She'd met him once when she first signed on as a donor, but couldn't remember his name. Jill called him Lawyer Guy and despite how shallow the label was, it had stuck in her mind. Seeing him there could not be good.

Lawyer Guy smiled, just a movement of the lips lacking any warmth, and stepped forward with an extended hand.

"Hello, Sarah."

She hesitantly took the proffered hand. "What's going on? Is the renter late?"

"Not exactly." Lawyer Guy turned and placed his briefcase on the nearest gurney, popped the locks, and extracted a sheaf of papers.

She scanned the documents and her frown deepened. It was the rental agreement.

Lawyer Guy held up a pen. "Don't worry, miss, your body is in perfect health. We just need to finalize some paperwork."

"I've already signed the contract. The return date is today."

"Of course," he said smoothly, "but you failed to initialize every section."

Sarah flipped through the document, confirming her initials were scribbled beneath every paragraph in the appointed space. "It all looks good to me."

"Page nine, paragraph four."

Sarah flipped back to the page and her heart sank. She thrust the papers at him, and this time her hand shook a little.

"That paragraph is optional. I chose not to sign it."

"I am afraid we need your signature now."

"Why?"

He held up the pen again. "Legalities, miss. I don't want to bore you with the details."

She shook her head and decided anger would work better than fear. "I know the contract. I know I don't have to sign this section, and I've always made it very clear I am not interested in permanent corporal transfer."

As she spoke, Lawyer Guy's smile faded. Sarah continued despite the growing fear that threatened to rob her projected anger of its force. "I signed a three month lease and expect my body to be returned as promised, today, in good working order per the signed agreement."

"Miss, there has been a development."

She held up one wrinkled hand. "Not my problem. I want my body. Now."

Lawyer Guy sighed and snapped his briefcase closed. "I am afraid we have a slight problem."

"What problem?"

"Follow me."

CHAPTER 6

L awyer Guy led Sarah through the plush halls
of the facility to the administrative offices, situated in the rear of the main building. They
took the elevator to the fourth floor where the senior officers worked. Sarah had never visited that
part of the facility.

What could possibly have happened? She thought
of the terrible damage done to Tawnya's body just a
couple days prior. Could it be something like that?
The thought filled her with dread and left a foul taste
in her mouth worse than the old crone's daily medi-
cine cocktail. All she wanted was to be herself again
and leave forever.

Lawyer Guy took her to the office of Michael
Fleischer, CEO. The secretary stationed outside the
office immediately waved them through the wide,
wood-paneled door.

Sarah paused in the doorway, taking in the view.
A full fireplace took up part of the right wall, with

several overstuffed chairs and two couches facing it. A complete wet bar lined the opposite wall. On the far side of the room, Mr. Fleischer's huge mahogany desk squatted before full-length windows that offered a spectacular view of the sprawling corporate facility with its many inter-connected buildings and beautifully manicured grounds. The facility perched atop one of Maryland's forested hills, with sweeping vistas of the surrounding countryside.

Mr. Fleischer rose from his overstuffed leather chair to meet them as they crossed the cavernous room. He was an overweight middle-aged man with salt-and-pepper hair and a clean shaven face. He wore an expensively tailored gray suit that matched his eyes.

He took Sarah's hands in both of his and said warmly, "Sarah, I'm glad you came."

"Thank you, sir," she said, her discomfort at facing the company CEO magnified by the fact that she'd had little choice but to come.

"Call me Michael." He directed her toward one of several leather chairs situated around his massive desk.

"What's going on, sir." Sarah asked as she gratefully settled her aching old bones into the soft chair.

While Lawyer Guy seated himself, Mr. Fleischer leaned back against the desk and fixed Sarah with a grave expression. "Sarah, you may not know this, but your renter is a very influential person. She couldn't be happier with the rental experience. She's a tremendous asset to Alterego in helping promote the work we do here."

"I am glad to hear that."

He smiled. "You have helped our efforts more than you know, and now we have an unexpected opportunity to achieve one of our principal objectives. With your help, we can do it, and in the same stroke we can silence some of our most dangerous critics in the legislature."

Sarah could not help but be moved by his words. She sat a little straighter despite a twinge in her back. "I'll do what I can to help, sir."

"I knew I could count on you."

Lawyer Guy passed the contract over again.

"I don't understand." She did not reach for the papers.

"Your renter has elected to exercise the permanent corporal transfer clause in the contract."

His words confirmed her worst fear. "With all due respect, sir, I did not agree to that clause. I've made it clear that I am not interested in—"

Mr. Fleischer interrupted, his smile harder, less friendly. "I understand this is a shock, Sarah, but your renter has agreed to pay a substantial settlement, from which you will receive a generous bonus."

"Thank you, sir, but I am not interested in a bonus. I just want my body back."

"Listen, Sarah," he said, frowning now. "You can help make history here. All we need is your cooperation."

"No, sir," Sarah said, growing angry at his condescension. "All you need is my body. I am not willing to give it away forever."

"It's not like you'd be an orphan. We have a dozen top-rated bodies you can choose from, bodies as young and fit as your own. You can be whoever you want to be, and become a very wealthy woman."

Sarah met Mr. Fleischer's penetrating gaze. "Have the owners of those bodies agreed to permanently surrender them to me?"

Mr. Fleischer smiled. "Thank you, Sarah. I know you'll be pleased with the arrangement." Lawyer Guy extended the contract and pen again.

"You didn't answer my question, sir."

Mr. Fleischer stood and waved a hand dismissively. "We'll get photos to you within the hour. You'll be given top priority for transfer."

"So it'll be a temporary transfer?"

"Don't worry, Sarah. We'll take care of everything."

"But I still lose my body and don't get a permanent replacement."

Mr. Fleischer sighed. "Listen, Sarah. We will arrange for a permanent transfer as soon as we possibly can. In the meantime, I promise you, we'll take care of you."

Sarah shook her head slowly, amazed at his audacity. In the same breath he was asking her to permanently, legally surrender her body to another person, without anything more tangible than his word that she'd ever own a body of her own again.

She couldn't do it. Just thinking about it made her shiver. What would she be? She'd be no one. Just a mental awareness shuffled between different bodies, the ultimate orphan.

Sarah shook her head. "I'm sorry, sir. But I'm afraid I have to decline your offer."

Mr. Fleischer's expression became dangerously neutral. He returned to his chair and leaned forward over the shining expanse of polished wood. "I thought you were smarter than this, Sarah. Do you have any idea how much money is at stake? How critical the timing is for this? What an opportunity this is?"

"It's not that. It's just—"

Mr. Fleischer spoke over her. "I don't accept excuses, Sarah. Only results."

"I'm sorry I can't help you."

"Think about it, Sarah. You don't want to make this hard on yourself."

"What do you mean?" Sarah had to fight to keep her voice calm. Mr. Fleischer's face was hard now, angry. Dangerous.

He pointed at her, at the decrepit old body she wore. "You enjoy great privileges here in this facility. Don't put those privileges at risk."

Sarah rocked back, barely fighting down a wave of terror at the implied threat. They couldn't leave her in this old body, could they?

Her hands started to shake and she clasped them in her lap to hide the telltale sign. All they really needed was a scribbled initial in the contract. If she refused, would they fill in the blank for her?

She could protest, take the matter to the police.

Would anyone believe her?

Would they give her the chance?

Mr. Fleischer sat behind his desk, watching her. She had no doubt that he could read her fear, was measuring it, calculating how far to push before she snapped.

How much more would it take? The thought of losing her body terrified her, but the alternative was even worse. She couldn't fathom being stuck in that old body until it died, of really *being* old.

Mr. Fleischer nodded as if reading her mind, a little smile on his lips. "You're as smart as I hoped." He pointed at Lawyer Guy, who slid the documents toward Sarah.

She looked at the pen, and the trembling in her hands worsened. What could she do?

I can't believe I'm really considering this!
What choice do I have?

"Do we understand each other?" Mr. Fleischer pressed.

Before she could reply, the intercom on the desk beeped and the secretary's voice rang through the office. "I am sorry for disturbing you, sir, but the auditor is here from the congressional oversight committee."

Mr. Fleischer glared at the intercom for a second before speaking. "Send him in immediately."

He rose as Lawyer Guy smoothly retrieved the documents from in front of Sarah and slipped them into his briefcase. "You'll excuse me, Sarah."

"Of course, sir." She staggered to her feet and headed for the door with all the speed propriety and her arthritic joints allowed.

The outer door of the office opened to admit the secretary and a balding, middle-aged man in a poorly cut suit that only seemed to magnify his pot belly. He squinted at Sarah through thick glasses.

Before Sarah could escape the room, Mr. Fleischer called out, "Sarah, think on what we discussed here. We will talk again soon."

As she slipped out the door, Mr. Fleischer greeted the auditor like a long lost friend. "Charles, so good of you to come."

"Thank you." The auditor had a thin, nasal voice.

"I can't wait to show you our facilities."

The heavy door closed, blocking the rest of the conversation. Sarah headed for the elevator, her heart aching with the choice she faced.

She all but ran for the transfer lab.

CHAPTER 7

On the way to the lab where she planned to do whatever it took to get transferred to another body, any other body, Sarah ran into the water aerobics instructor. The woman took her arm despite her protests, and led her down to the pool. It was time to exercise the old body and Sarah was on the clock, so she had no choice. She could not risk giving Mr. Fleischer any more leverage against her.

She tried to exercise, but her old body was shaky, disoriented as it reacted to the adrenaline pumping through its old veins in response to her fears. How could they do this to her? All she wanted was her body back, and then she'd be gone forever. She'd saved enough money for the early buy-out.

Could they really take her body away? The thought was so terrifying, it left a gaping hole in her gut that sapped her strength and pushed her to the verge of tears. She'd been able to handle being a donor only because of the dollar figures clouding her vision. When not on the clock, she got to use young, fit bodies that were decent temporary replacements of her own. Could she be satisfied in one of them forever?

She shivered to think how close she'd come to caving to Mr. Fleischer's demands, and doubted she'd do any better the next time they met. Now that she had a little distance and time to think about it, she could not agree to give up her body forever.

Could. Not. Do. It.

So what could she do? She had no illusion that he'd accept her denial. He'd bully her until he got what he wanted. Or, if she gave him too much trouble, would he forge her signature and lock her away?

He could do it. There was a holding area in the sub-basement, referred to only as the 'vault,' where they held convicts whose bodies were used as extras for donors while their own bodies were being rented. She'd never been into the vault, but didn't doubt there was room in there for her.

No one would ever know. Only the head surgeon and her assistants entered the vault. Sarah doubted that even Tomas had ever been in there. She had no family, no one to raise the alarm if she vanished. They could lock her away forever and use her body as they saw fit.

She could not escape. Realization struck like a slap in the face. She was a prisoner. No, a slave to Alterego. They hid the fact with hefty bonuses, but the truth of it stole her strength and she nearly fainted. She barely managed to get to the edge of the pool as her aged body shook in response to the mental anguish.

"Are you all right." a young attendant asked. She helped Sarah out of the pool and wrapped her in towels, watching her closely. The last thing the company wanted was a damaged renter's body.

"I'm fine," Sarah managed. "Just don't have it in me today."

The young woman smiled at her like she was really an old lady and steadied her on the trip back to the locker room.

This can't be happening.

Then a ray of hope illuminated her soul and drove the near-panic back a few steps. She smiled as the idea took root.

Of course. The government auditor was there in the facility. She'd heard something about the visit the other day, but hadn't paid much attention. Apparently there were powerful critics of the corporation lobbying congress to abolish the practice of human body rentals. The debates were heated, and the auditor, along with a medical team, were visiting the facility to prepare a report for the congressional committee handling the issue.

The auditor could help. All Sarah had to do was explain the situation to him. He could force Mr. Fleischer to honor the terms of the contract, or threaten congressional action if he didn't comply.

Sarah nearly laughed with relief. Mr. Fleischer had picked the wrong day to threaten her. Her resolve firmed with renewed hope. She would escape this place on her terms.

CHAPTER 8

Sarah awoke and sat up. She glanced down at the young body she now wore, wrapped in a hospital gown, and breathed a huge sigh of relief. She closed her eyes for a moment and savored the feeling of youth and health. It had never felt better to get out of that decrepit, old biddy.

She dressed quickly, grateful that she again wore the same model she'd been using in recent days. It felt almost natural after so much time with it. New bodies were always a little strange at first, a little awkward, as if her consciousness needed a little time to fit into the new physical form.

This one gave her very little trouble. She'd grown used to its balance, height, weight, and proportions, even though nothing felt as good as her own skin. When she returned to it after a rental, it was like slipping into her old, favorite jeans that had contoured themselves perfectly to her from countless hours of use.

Would she ever get it back?

Yes! She strode from the transfer lab, but instead of heading for the exit to the rest of the facility like normal, she turned left and moved deeper into the transfer complex. Mr. Fleischer had said they were going to show the auditor the facility, so he had to be down there somewhere. All she needed was a few minutes of his time.

The transfer facility was extensive, with a dozen transfer labs, medical facilities that included a level II trauma center, more than one hundred lavishly outfitted individual rooms for renter bodies when they were not being exercised, staff rooms, and more. Hidden underground beneath the rental offices, it burrowed six stories down into the bedrock.

After half an hour of fruitless searching in which she didn't dare ask anyone for help, she decided to return to the lobby near the bank of elevators. No matter where he might be squirreled away, the auditor would pass that way eventually.

Within ten minutes, the double doors at the far end of the hall swung open for a group of people. At seeing them, Sarah's heart sank. Mr. Fleischer strode at the front of the group, smiling like the Cheshire cat.

'Conan' followed him.

The tall, handsome, hugely muscled body was the number one male renter. Known as a super-athlete,

it had been rented for many different sporting events
and had always performed remarkably.

Flanking 'Conan' were Dr. Maerwynn, the head
surgeon, and Jill, who now wore a voluptuous young
body that Sarah recognized as 'A Night to Remember.' She was hanging on Conan's arm, wearing an
athletic outfit that accentuated her spectacular figure.

As the group drew nearer, Sarah started in surprise as she recognized Conan's face.

The auditor.

Sarah's hopes fell. The auditor was beaming like
the boy who had just scored the winning touchdown.
His eyes moved constantly from his reflection that
kept pace in the hall-length mirrors, to Jill who was
smiling at him like he was the center of her universe.

His weak face didn't really fit Conan's head, looking stretched and unnatural, but he didn't seem to notice. He grinned and flexed his biceps in the mirror.
Jill ran a hand down his arm and leaned against him
to whisper something in his ear.

He laughed loudly and wrapped an arm around
her slender waist. "This is the most amazing thing
I've ever seen. How is it possible?"

"The science is a closely guarded secret, as you
can imagine, but Dr. Maerwynn will cover the process at a high level in the conference room this afternoon," Mr. Fleischer said with a wide smile. "But first,

why don't you go take that model for a spin? We have extensive fitness facilities. Jill will show you around."

The group paused at the elevators and Mr. Fleischer cast a hard look at Sarah, but did not speak. She stood mute, rooted in place until the elevator doors closed behind them.

Then she fell into a nearby padded chair and buried her head in her hands. This could not be happening. The auditor would never help her now. Mr. Fleischer had bought the man just like he was trying to buy her.

He'd seen her. Did he suspect what she was trying to do? What did it matter? He'd effectively cut off the only hope of escape.

"Sarah, are you all right?"

She glanced up in surprise to see Tomas approaching, his face concerned.

"Are you crying?"

She wiped her face with one hand and lied, "No. Just resting."

Tomas gave her a long look. "Do you need anything?"

She sniffled. "Yeah, a miracle."

"What?"

"Never mind." She jumped out of the chair and ran for the elevator.

Tomas watched her go, his expression grim.

CHAPTER 9

Mr. Fleischer leaned back in the tall executive chair behind his massive desk and regarded Dr. Maerwynn and the technician, Tomas.

"How is it going with our auditor?"

Dr. Maerwynn said, "He is weak and easily manipulated." She brushed her shoulder-length black hair from her strong face. With the artfully applied make-up, she still looked to be in her twenties, an illusion reinforced by her young, trim physique.

"And the medical evaluation team?"

"In the lab now with one of my assistants. They should be gone by mid-afternoon."

"Good, good. Everything is coming together."

Tomas said, "There is one small complication, sir. With the bodies sequestered for the audit examinations, we're short two for today's rotation."

"I thought we accounted for the audit in our numbers."

"We did," Dr. Maerwynn said, "but the prison is late sending us the latest inmate transfers."

"Shall I send the dispossessed to the vault." Tomas asked.

Dr. Maerwynn said. "No. They're not prepared for that. It would raise too many questions."

Mr. Fleischer sat back in his chair, his face expressionless as he considered the situation. Tomas said hesitantly into the silence, "There is one other option, sir. The dolls are ready."

Dr. Maerwynn shook her head, "I'd rather that information not circulate yet."

"Can't we just keep them sedated?" Mr. Fleischer asked.

"No," said the doctor. "The drugs only work on the bodies. Once the souls are free, they'd be conscious within minutes."

"Then what do you recommend?"

She grimaced. "We have to use the dolls."

"I don't need this today," Mr. Fleischer growled.

"I see no other option."

"Very well. Do it." He leaned forward and fixed both of the others with his hard stare. "But keep it contained."

Tomas said, "Shall I pick two random donors?"

"No." Mr. Fleischer considered for a moment and then smiled. "Use Sarah and Jill."

Tomas looked surprised, and Dr. Maerwynn said, "Jill is a good choice. That woman won't care what she gets. But are you sure about Sarah? She's still resisting the full corporal transfer."

"Oh, yes," Mr. Fleischer said with a grin. "I'm sure. This will provide the last bit of leverage we need to bring her into line."

"I'll see it done," Tomas said.

"Good. And make sure we get that convict body ready for her next jump."

CHAPTER 10

Sarah couldn't remember most of the afternoon. It passed in a blur as she struggled with the terrifying dilemma. Despite her best efforts, she could not think of a way to escape the situation with her identity intact.

She could run away, but that wouldn't help much. She wouldn't be old, but she still wouldn't have her body, and she couldn't bring herself to steal someone else's.

She didn't like Mr. Fleischer, but did not doubt he'd pay the huge promised bonus. One thing Alterego was very good at was paying its donors handsomely. With how badly he wanted her to accept the permanent corporal transfer, she could walk away very wealthy.

Was it worth torturing herself so much? By the amount of money rich old men and women were willing to pay for the chance at even temporary youth, it seemed she was the only person who felt her own, original body was worth holding on to.

She could not change the way she felt.

So what was she to do?

She barely summed up enough courage to undergo the transfer back into that same old body to take it through its afternoon exercise routine. All through the two hour session, she watched the clock move with agonizing slowness.

"Sarah, what's wrong." Jill asked at one point. "You're moving like a zombie."

Sarah managed a weak smile. "Just preoccupied."

"Why are you still wearing that old thing? I thought you were getting yourself back today."

Fighting back tears, Sarah told Jill about the situation. She was startled when Jill said, "You lucky gal."

"How is this lucky?"

"You're going to be rich!"

"Didn't you hear me? They want to take my body forever."

Jill shrugged. "But they said they'll give you another one, right?"

Sarah nodded.

"Just make sure it passes the full medical screening. Don't want to take one with cancer or something."

"I don't want to take anything," Sarah said angrily. "I just want to be me."

"So just tell them."

"I did. They won't let me." She leaned closer. "I think they're planning to force me to take it."

"So take it." Jill regarded Sarah for a moment. "I worry about you sometimes. You just don't seem to get it. Take the money. You'll be set for life. The company will take care of you. You won't have to worry about anything."

"I don't trust the company."

"Why not? Haven't they paid you more money than any sane person has a right to deserve?"

"Yes."

"Then what's there not to trust?"

Sarah shrugged. "Don't you ever feel trapped here? Like a prisoner?"

"It's not always about you, Sarah."

"What?"

"You're so stuck on yourself," Jill said with surprising heat. "Here you've got it made. You get paid a ton. You've got no responsibilities. Alterego can take care of your entire life for you, and it's not enough. You're so selfish sometimes."

Sarah stared at her friend, totally shocked. "Jill, I . . ."

Jill waved her to silence. "Think about the rest of us for once, Sarah. What will happen to us if you rock the boat and wreck things?"

"I didn't—"

Jill spoke right over her. "If you mess things up, we'll all be out of work. We'd all have to figure out how to take care of ourselves. That would be really mean, Sarah."

"I don't want to hurt anyone."

"Good, then take the deal. Everyone will be happier."

Not me.

After the workout, Sarah would have run back to the transfer lab if it wouldn't have risked giving her old body a heart attack. Despite how much she wanted out of it, dying was not the way to do it.

Tomas was waiting for them as usual, but his normal smile was missing. In fact, he looked rather grim. On top of everything else, his expression sent a chill sense of foreboding crawling down her spine. With a shock, Sarah realized he looked strikingly similar to Mr. Fleischer, especially with that look on his face. He could have almost passed for the man's son.

Tomas helped Jill up onto her gurney and she asked, "So where's my next body?"

Only then did Sarah realize the other two gurneys that normally held the bodies they would transfer to stood empty. The feeling of foreboding blossomed into full blown fear.

"They're coming," Tomas said as he prepared the pre-transfer injection.

Jill grinned wickedly, a singularly disturbing expression on her aged face. "You're going to sneak in that sexy little number for me, aren't you?"

"It will be little," Tomas said with a rather forced grin.

Jill laughed and then cast a coy look at him. "I'm not sure it'll be enough, but we'll see. I might let you take me out."

Tomas' only reply was to jab the needle into her arm and inject the tranquilizer.

When he turned to Sarah, he was frowning. Wild fears popped into her head. What was he doing? Was he going to kill them? The idea would usually have seemed ludicrous, but she could not bring herself to laugh it off.

"Hold on a minute," she said as he prepared her arm.

"Don't move." He leaned close, his gaze so intense Sarah pressed herself back into the bed. "I am sorry, Sarah. This will be . . . strange."

"You're making me nervous."

He managed a weak smile. "Just remember. I'll be there. I'll look after you."

"What's going on?"

He jabbed the needle home.

"I promise. You'll be safe."

The words looked forced, as if he didn't believe them.

She tried to push his hand away, but moved too late. He injected the tranquilizer.

"I am sorry."

His words faded to blackness.

CHAPTER 11

onsciousness returned like a bucket of icy water dashed across her mind. Sarah started awake and tried to sit up, but her body felt wrong, heavy. She frowned and blinked. Her eyelids moved slowly, as if she were still half asleep.

What's wrong with me?

She'd never had so much trouble waking up in a new body. Only then did her surroundings register, and she stared. She was not lying in the transfer lab. The room looked like a lounge, but something was wrong. Everything was surrounded by rainbow halos, and it was all . . . huge.

It was like she'd been dumped into some gigantic movie set and she was a hobbit, or maybe even Thumbelina. The room seemed like a vast open cavern, filled with the biggest furniture she'd ever heard of, complete with an impossibly huge television hanging on the far wall.

She glanced to her left. Her head turned very slowly, as if she'd lain unmoving for weeks and her muscles had stiffened. She sat on some kind of gigantic sofa in the crazy-huge lounge. She could get a dozen friends and play a game of football on that sofa. Who would make such a monstrosity, and why?

Maybe something had gone wrong with that last transfer? Her sight was messed up, and she could not smell anything. Could it be a hallucination? That would almost be better. Dr. Maerwynn would fix it. Everyone said the doctor was brilliant.

She felt as if every muscle had fallen asleep and hadn't started tingling yet, so she glanced down.

Definitely hallucinating.

She stared in abstract fascination at her doll-like body sitting in the fold of the gigantic sofa. She'd never imagined what a doll would look like from its own eyes, but if she ever tried, it would be this. The details were amazing. It all looked so real. She tried to move her arm, and the little china hand raised an inch. She'd never had such vivid dreams.

Sarah turned to the right to glance down the far expanse of the couch. Another doll sat beside her, dressed in a pretty pink dress, with its little china hands clutching a tiny television remote.

Sarah started to smile at the life-size china doll, but it turned toward her. It wore Jill's face.

A terrifying suspicion began dawning, something so absurd it couldn't be real.

The Jill-doll smiled. The china doll face actually smiled, and it spoke with a voice that might have been Jill's if she'd just inhaled a helium balloon. "Isn't this incredible!"

Sarah tried to recoil, but her body did not react. She'd managed to move her one hand and her face, but the rest of it still seemed asleep.

"Get away from me," she shouted, her voice also pitched helium high.

The Jill-doll laughed, a flat, tinny sound that made Sarah shiver. "I can't, Sarah. Only the hands move."

"Wake up, Sarah," she said to herself, tilting her head back to look up at the ceiling that soared what looked like half a mile overhead. "Just wake up! It's just a transfer nightmare."

"Sarah, look at me," Jill said in her high pitched doll voice.

"No. I'm dreaming, that's all."

"Sarah, don't be an idiot. This is wonderful."

The absurdity of that statement brought Sarah's gaze back to the Jill-doll, and drove a dagger of fear into her cold porcelain heart. Even in a dream, she'd never make Jill so ridiculous. Only the real Jill could do that.

"Check this out," Jill-doll said. She lifted her little china hands, pointed the remote at the far wall, and pushed one of its three buttons. On the far wall, the television came to life.

Jill-doll laughed her little laugh. "Already pre-set to my favorite show. This is great."

"You're insane."

"Is everyone all right." Tomas' voice boomed like a thunderclap from across the room.

Sarah slow-turned her head as an impossibly huge Tomas crossed the room and dropped to one knee beside the giant couch, his head bigger than her entire body.

"Please tell me I'm hallucinating," Sarah begged in her helium-high doll voice.

He shook his head sadly. "I tried to warn you."

"Warn me." Sarah shouted, terror turning to anger, heightened by her silly voice. "You said it would be strange. How is this strange?! We passed strange back in Oz. This is . . . is . . ."

Tomas held up a hand mirror to show her reflection in full china doll glory, complete with yellow sun dress and matching slippers. Her fake doll hair was gathered on both sides of her head, and stood out almost horizontal. Seeing her own face staring out of that china doll body drove home the truth of the nightmare.

She would have fainted if the doll body would allow it, but when it didn't work, she closed her eyes instead.

"I just won't look. I'll wake up soon and it'll all be a dream."

"Sarah," Tomas' voice rolled over her. "Look at me."

"No."

"Sarah, what's gotten into you?" Jill-doll asked.

That made her look. She slow-swiveled her head around to meet Jill-doll's tiny gaze. "Have you not been paying attention? They've turned us into dolls!"

"Not exactly," Tomas said. "Your souls were transferred to the dolls just like they have been to other bodies dozens of times."

"Impossible."

"Really?" Tomas asked with a hint of a smile. "You're living it."

"It's a nightmare. That's all."

Jill-doll said, "Get a grip. This is great. I can watch TV all day like this. What a vacation."

Sarah turned back to Tomas, who regarded Jill with a sad, pitying expression.

"How is this possible?"

"You've been lied to."

"No, I've been turned into a doll."

"We need to talk." Tomas gently lifted Sarah and stood. The room tilted and shifted as she soared up into the air in his hands. At least the doll body didn't suffer vertigo.

Tomas crossed to the far side of the room and sat Sarah carefully on a little shelf high on the wall. He glanced back at Jill, but she didn't even seem to have noticed they'd left. She sat staring at the giant TV, and her little doll laugh echoed across the room.

"Why don't you want Jill to hear this?"

"She's not ready."

"Ready for what?"

"The truth."

CHAPTER 12

Everything you know about Alterego is a lie."

"You're saying old rich people aren't really renting our bodies?"

Tomas waved a dismissive hand. "That's just a carefully crafted cover. The so-called technology that allows Dr. Maerwynn to transfer your consciousness between bodies is just an elaborate smoke-and-mirrors. It doesn't exist."

"Something exists. I got turned into a doll, remember?"

Tomas regarded her for a second. "You may find the truth hard to believe."

"I'm a doll. How much weirder can it get?"

Tomas managed a little smile. "Dr. Maerwynn is not a doctor at all. She's a Facetaker, one of a very small number of people who have the power to remove a person's soul and place it into a different body."

If she hadn't just woken up as a china doll, Sarah would have laughed in his face. "You're saying it's magic?"

"That's as good a term for it as any right now."

"Are we on candid camera?"

Tomas barked a laugh. "If only."

"Let's assume I believe you. How is it possible?"

Tomas shrugged. "I don't know exactly. I'm not a facetaker, but I know that they've been around since the dawn of time. Their ancient power has been a carefully guarded secret for millennia."

"That doesn't make sense. They can't keep a secret by publicizing it. The truth will get out eventually."

"Probably. That doesn't seem to bother them any more."

"They'll be arrested, or worse."

"Maybe not. There are other things going on here, masked by the rental company."

"Like what?"

"Like the vault."

"What about it? They keep the convicts transferred from the prison there, right?"

"Yes, but the vault is huge, and it's not a prison in the traditional sense."

"What do you mean?"

"The convict donor program includes about a hundred convicts, but the vault can store thousands of souls."

Sarah tried to frown, but she wasn't entirely sure it worked. "Why?"

"It's a gathering place. Under cover of the rental agency program, they're gathering souls here."

"Why?"

"I'm not sure. I can think of a couple of possible reasons, and none of them are good."

Sarah held up one little doll hand. "This is too much Tomas. Why are you telling me all this?"

Tomas gave her a very serious look. "How badly do you want your body back?"

"More than anything."

"What are you willing to do to get it?"

"Whatever it takes," she assured him instantly, and she meant it.

Tomas nodded. "You're ready, that's why."

"There's more to it than that."

"Yes, but I've told you what you need to know for now."

"What do we do next?"

Tomas lifted her from the shelf. "Now I prove to you that I'm telling the truth."

CHAPTER 13

T omas carried Sarah from the lounge and she was surprised to recognize the halls of the transfer lab. Everything was familiar and foreign at the same time. The vast sizes and rainbow light surrounding everything turned the normal into something frightfully alien. With the knowledge she now possessed, an ominous sense of foreboding overshadowed the entire scene.

Could she trust Tomas?

Could she *not* trust him?

Tomas moved through the halls briskly, and when another white-coated attendant stepped into the corridor, he slipped Sarah into one of his pockets and whispered, "Be quiet."

Sarah, her face pressed against the white cloth of his pocket, did not have to be told twice. The peril of her current situation was driven home by how easily he hid her from sight.

If they want to, they could lock me away forever and no one would ever know. No one could ever find me.

She was completely at Tomas' mercy. Sarah pushed aside the fears that multiplied with the thought. She could trust Tomas, she had to. The alternative was just too terrifying.

A moment later, Tomas pulled her from his pocket. He stood in a transfer station, although this one held only two gurneys. One lay empty, waiting for the donor, while the other held a motionless body covered by a white sheet and the ever-present, claustrophobic life support unit clamped around the head.

Tomas moved to the corner of the room and positioned Sarah carefully on a high shelf. He placed a roll of paper towels and a stack of linens in front of her, arranged to hide her from view.

"What are you doing?" she asked, happy that her helium-high doll voice masked the squeak of fear in her words.

If he left her like this, it might be months before anyone noticed her.

"Can you still see the gurneys?"

"Yes."

"Good." Tomas stepped back, critically eyed the shelf where he'd hidden her, and nodded. "You should be safe there."

"Safe from what?"

He stepped closer, "You must remain silent. If they hear you," he glanced around nervously, "If they hear you . . . well, let's just say I don't think I'd be able to save you."

The open fear on his face sent a shiver of dread through her sleeping doll body. "Maybe this isn't such a good idea."

"You have to see."

"I believe you, really."

"That's not enough. You need to *know*."

Tomas headed for the door, but paused with one hand on the handle. "Remember. No matter what happens, you must remain silent. I'll return for you after they're gone."

Then he slipped out of the room and left her alone. The closing of the door seemed unusually loud in the silent transfer station.

Sarah peered through the narrow gap toward the two gurneys in the center of the room. There were many transfer stations, more than were strictly necessary to handle the donor transfers. Some were not used for weeks at a time.

Had Tomas lied to her? He'd been acting a little weird lately. Had he decided to kidnap her and keep her as his own little toy?

Now I'm being ridiculous.

She had been turned into a doll, though. No technology she'd ever heard of could do that. Could it really be magic? What else could it be? Questions whirled through her mind, but she did not know enough to figure out any answers.

Ten minutes later, the door to the room opened and two people entered. Sarah was so relieved to see someone, anyone, that she nearly called out to them. Only Tomas' grave warning made her hold her tongue.

She recognized the newcomers. The serious young blonde in the white lab coat was one of Dr. Maerwynn's three medical assistants, named Almeda. The old woman was worn by Tawnya, the donor whose body had been injured by the careless renter.

Almeda helped Tawnya up onto the empty gurney. "Your body is healing well."

"I can't wait to get back into it," Tawnya said with a glance at the sheet-covered gurney beside her.

"You will experience some pain, but we must start physical therapy today for optimal recovery."

"I can take it."

"Very good." Almeda injected Tawnya with the pre-op tranquilizer.

Despite all the unknowns that clamored in her head, making her want to scream with frustrated fear and pull at her fake hair, Sarah watched with unblinking interest. She'd never actually seen a corporal transfer.

She'd always been tranquilized prior to the operation, and no one but Dr. Maerwynn or her assistants were allowed in the room during the actual transfer operation. To protect the copyrighted technology, they were told.

Almeda extracted from a squat cupboard near the door one of the bulky life support units, which she clamped around Tawnya's sleeping head. Once it rested over her like a metal monster that had swallowed her head and neck in a single bite, Almeda flipped a couple of switches. The unit beeped twice, a few lights blinked, and its quiet hum filled the room.

The door opened then, and Dr. Maerwynn entered the room, followed by a male technician wheeling a tall piece of machinery. He plugged it in, positioned it at the head of Tawnya's gurney, and silently withdrew.

As Almeda moved to the machine and began typing swiftly at the attached keyboard, Sarah studied the unit. She'd never seen it before, but assumed it was the actual transfer unit she'd heard so much about.

She'd expected something more.

The simple rectangular base stood three feet tall and two feet on each side. Made out of shining stainless steel, the outer shell was unmarked except for bright red letters emblazoned along one side that proclaimed, "SOTRUN 2." Atop the steel base sat the keyboard with its small monitor, while a thick metal post rose to a height of six feet like a crane. A standard white, multi-segmented arm extended out the front, looking just like similar ones she'd seen so often in dentist offices and hospital rooms.

Instead of a light or computer monitor, the arm held a silvery piece of machinery that looked a lot like one of those vision testing apparatuses used by optometrists. The difference was that this one was held horizontal, and some of the myriad knobs and circular viewports looked jagged. Sarah winced at the thought of that contraption pressing down against her eyes.

Dr. Maerwynn positioned the odd contraption over the life support unit encasing Tawnya's head, and locked the two together with a series of clamps.

"Is everything ready?"

"Yes, ma'am," Almeda said without looking up from her work at the machine.

"Good."

Dr. Maerwynn slipped her hands into a pair of slots set in the side of the optometry-like device. Situated like that, her hands would be positioned directly above Tawnya's mouth.

Although the transfer unit looked nothing like what Sarah had imagined, she watched with growing anticipation. Surprisingly, Dr. Maerwynn closed her eyes, took a deep breath, and her face settled into a mask of concentration. She opened her eyes and they started to glow like purple LED screens.

"Activate," she breathed, her voice filled with anticipation.

Almeda typed a quick command on the keyboard, then struck the Enter key with a hard slap.

The hum of machinery increased and purple light flickered out the ports where Dr. Maerwynn's hands remained hidden. It also flashed weakly from behind the opaque shield covering Tawnya's face.

Then Sarah heard a loud, metallic click, and the old body Tawnya wore twitched hard, as if she'd been hit with an electrical current. Dr. Maerwynn threw her head back in silent ecstasy and, in a husky voice that was completely out of place in an operating theater said, "Release the clamps."

Moving with practiced efficiency, Almeda uncoupled the transfer machine from Tawnya's life support unit, and Dr. Maerwynn lifted it away, her hands still stuck inside. The purple glow had faded, but the unit trailed some kind of weird, rainbow mist as they repositioned it above Tawnya's injured young body.

Sarah watched with growing confusion. This looked nothing like what she expected, and Dr. Maerwynn's actions in particular made her deeply nervous. Perhaps Tomas' claims that the technology wasn't entirely real held some truth, although she didn't see anything overtly magical about the process.

There had to be an explanation for the purple glow. Still, the rest of the operation looked wrong at a fundamental level that she couldn't quite put her fingers on.

Down in the transfer lab, the two women clamped the strange transfer device to the other life support unit, and the purple glow began flashing again from within the machines. Dr. Maerwynn bowed her head over the unit like a mourner over a casket, and her eyes again began to glow in that freakish way.

Almeda typed furiously on the keyboard, her eyes glued to the little display. After a moment she nodded and said, " Brain waves stabilized. Engage."

At the same time, Tawnya's entire body twitched like she was startling out of a sound sleep.

Dr. Maerwynn removed her hands from the unit, unclamped it from the life support box encasing Tawnya's head, and pushed it back toward the door. Her expression had settled back to professional calm, and Sarah struggled to reconcile the doctor's strange behavior during the transfer. Maybe she was just someone who really got into her work?

Almeda moved to Tawnya and began checking vitals, but Dr. Maerwynn strode from the room. A moment later, the same male technician entered, helped Almeda remove and stow the life support unit, then wheeled the transfer apparatus away.

Tawnya, who slept peacefully under the lingering effects of the tranquilizer, looked fine, like nothing had happened. Still, Sarah shivered in her china doll body. She'd lain docile and unconcerned countless times through the exact same procedure, and now she felt like she understood even less than ever about what really went on in the lab.

How did that simple-looking machine affect the full transfer of a person's consciousness to another body?

For the first time, Sarah began to fear the answer.

CHAPTER 14

Within minutes Tawnya awoke, blissfully unaware. She chatted excitedly with Almeda about how wonderful it was to be back in her own body, despite her injuries, and discussed the upcoming physical therapy.

Tomas arrived a moment later and helped Tawnya into a wheelchair. He didn't even glance in Sarah's direction before wheeling Tawnya from the room. A second staff member came for the old renter body and wheeled it away.

Sarah waited impatiently for Almeda to leave so Tomas could come retrieve her, but the woman only moved to the work bench directly below Sarah's hiding place, out of her range of vision.

A moment later the door opened again and a pretty young woman in a baggy orange correctional facility jumpsuit entered the room, followed by a uniformed officer.

Almeda pointed at the empty gurney. The convict sat on the edge of the bed and glanced around the room nervously.

"Whatcha gonna do to me?"

"Lie down. This won't hurt."

The convict complied, but repeated her question.

"Don't worry," Almeda said, "you've volunteered to be part of an exciting new technology."

"I aint signed up for nothing." The convict tried to sit up, but the officer held her down and growled something threatening.

Almeda produced a needle and swiftly injected the pre-op tranquilizer.

The convict yelped. ""Ow. Hey, I got rights. I . . ." Her voice trailed off as the fast-acting tranquilizer pushed her into oblivion.

"Thank you," Almeda told the officer, who retreated from the room.

As soon as he left, Almeda positioned herself over the convict's head. Sarah tried to frown as Almeda grasped the sleeping woman's face and dug her fingers under the lower edges of her jaw.

Almeda's eyes began to glow just as Dr. Maerwynn's had. Purple fire ignited across her fingers, and they sank into the skin along the convict's jaw.

Sarah watched in confusion and growing concern as the purple fire rippled up along the convict's jawline. If Almeda was preparing for a transfer, why hadn't she attached the life support unit? Where was the SOTRUN unit? What was that crazy purple fire?

Then the prone woman's face began to peel away from the skull with a wet, sucking sound like a boot being pulled out of thick mud. A gap appeared between the woman's face and the skull near the jaw, and widened up toward her forehead until half her face was leveraged up. Then with a loud pop, the face came free, complete with her nose, and with eyeballs trailing ragged nerve clusters.

Sarah bit back an anguished cry as she watched with stunned disbelief. Almeda had just ripped that convict's face right off!

Lacking the concealing protection of the machinery, Sarah witnessed in full, horrifying detail as trailers of flesh dropped away and the face thinned, the eyes compressing into half-spheres. By the time Almeda raised the face to shoulder height, it looked like a translucent, shimmering full-face mask trailing tendrils of rainbow smoke.

As Almeda threw her head back in silent ecstasy, mirroring Dr. Maerwynn's reaction when she operated on Tawnya, Sarah fought to keep from screaming. The truth struck her so hard that had she had command of her stomach, she would have puked all over the room.

Tomas was right, although he hadn't prepared her for the awful reality of it. She didn't know the convict, but couldn't bear to see such torture being inflicted on the unsuspecting woman.

How many times had they ripped pieces of Sarah out of whatever body she possessed and she'd lain innocent under their hands? She wanted to scream at Almeda to stop, wanted to claw at the creature's eyes, but she couldn't do anything while stuck in the doll body, and was forced to silently witness the horrible procedure. On the gurney, the skin where the convict's face had been removed settled into a smooth, blank mask, flowing together like water in a pond.

Only when Almeda stood holding the convict's translucent face free of the woman's body did Sarah realize something else was wrong. There was no other body in the room to transfer the face to.

Almeda placed the face on a counter and extracted a rectangular box from a cabinet. It looked like a safety deposit box, about as long as a person's forearm, and half as wide. She flipped open the lid, revealing a blank, padded interior, and dropped the face inside.

Almeda closed the lid and latched it. Then she covered the faceless body with a sheet and attached a life support unit over the head and neck. A moment later, a staff member arrived to wheel the body away. With the life support unit's opaque shield blocking their view of the missing face, they had no way of knowing what mutated person they were pushing from the room.

With the face gone, the front of the skull had ended up looking a lot like a blank mannequin head, the front covered with smooth skin, broken only by a narrow slit where the nose should go. Strangely, the skull looked intact, as if the jaw and facial bone structure remained, although somewhat flattened.

Sarah couldn't grasp how that could be possible, unless maybe Almeda had only pulled off the soft tissue atop the actual bones? The shimmering face masks looked pretty thin, but how would the muscles retain their shape? How . . . she didn't even know how to phrase the next question. The entire concept was just too new for her to hazard any rational guesses.

Just as Almeda took up the box that held the convict's face, the door opened and another of Dr. Maerwynn's assistants entered the room. Mai Luan was a slender Chinese-American who had inherited the best of both ancestries. She wore her silky, black hair long, tied back to accentuate her delicate features. Her face looked more

American than Chinese, and she stood average height, with a slender, athletic build.

"I'll take that," Mai Luan said without preamble as she collected the box containing the convict's face.

"Of course," Almeda said quickly. "I was just coming to find you."

"I bet you were." Mai Luan regarded her with an icy, unfriendly look. "Stay out of the vault unless I send for you."

Without waiting for a reply, she tucked the gruesome package under one arm and strode from the room.

Almeda scowled at the closed door and whispered, "I hate you." Then she glanced around the room, and for a second Sarah feared she might have made some kind of noise to give herself away. But Almeda did not notice her up on the high shelf and, after straightening her hair, left the room.

Sarah stared after her, filled with icy horror. *They took the convict's face and didn't give her another body.*

Mai Luan was taking her to the vault. That reminded her of something Tomas had said about the vault.

It's not a prison in the traditional sense.

Sarah wished she could cry. They were going to lock the convict away in the vault with no body, stuck in that little box.

Would she die? Would she wake up in that tiny coffin?

Would they do the same to Sarah?

The thought was so terrifying she wanted to scream. How could she have lived in that nightmare place and think for a moment that it was great?

Tomas arrived then and pulled her down from the shelf. "Are you all right?"

"I saw it," she told him in a voice that shook so badly she could barely get the words out.

"Come. It's time for your next transfer."

"Wait," Sarah shrieked in her little doll voice. "I can't. I can't go through that again. Not now, not after seeing it."

"Do you want to stay like that forever?"

"No!"

"Then you have no choice." Tomas held her up to eye level. "Remember, you can't let them know that you know. You have to pretend everything is normal."

Sarah laughed her little helium laugh. "I'm a china doll! How can this be normal?"

Tomas smiled. "It's all a matter of perspective."

He returned to the lounge to collect Jill, who was still watching television. As he carried them both to the transfer station where their next bodies waited, Jill gushed over how wonderful the experience had been.

"I hope we get to do that again," Jill said. "Did you realize dolls don't get tired? They don't need to eat or use the bathroom."

Her little china doll face beamed. "I could watch TV all day without having to stop. Isn't that great?"

"You're insane."

"You're so old-fashioned," Jill retorted. "This is the future. Just think, everything taken care of, no need to do anything but relax. It's the perfect life."

How could Sarah possibly reply to that?

Doctor Maerwynn herself waited for them in the transfer station where two sheet-covered bodies lay on gurneys.

"Well, ladies, how are you doing." she asked.

Sarah could not speak. In her mind, she again saw Almeda holding the convict's face aloft as flesh slid away, her expression exultant.

Hers had been the face of a demon.

Thankfully Jill was there, and she did not hesitate. "It was awesome. What a technological breakthrough!"

"Thank you," Dr. Maerwynn said with a smile. "I'm glad you enjoyed it."

"I loved it."

"You are a unique woman. I'm sure you will continue to play an important role here at Alterego for a long time to come."

Jill beamed.

"And what about you, Sarah?"

Sarah refused to meet Dr. Maerwynn's gaze. She managed to say, "It was . . . interesting."

"Quite an understatement." Dr. Maerwynn stepped closer and drew Sarah's gaze, her face no longer friendly. "Remember what you saw."

She knows!

How could she?

Sarah was just glad the little doll body made it difficult to show her expression. She stammered, "I don't understand."

"You have a meeting with Mr. Fleischer after this transfer. I recommend you remember this experience."

Oh, that. Sarah sagged against Tomas' hand despite the clear threat. Take the deal Mr. Fleischer offered, or be stuck as a doll forever.

"I will," she said.

"Very good." Dr. Maerwynn pointed at a nearby counter. "Tomas, leave them there."

Tomas obeyed and then left the room. Dr. Maerwynn approached, "In these doll bodies, our normal tranquilizers won't work." She wrapped a dark cloth around their heads. "This may feel a little strange, but I promise it won't hurt."

Fear spiked in Sarah's heart. She knew what was coming. She had to let it happen, but with her eyes covered, she could not help but see in her mind the nameless woman's face pulling free, trailing rainbow smoke.

Fingers slipped under the cloth and wrapped around her little china face. Sarah barely bit back a scream. Panic threatened to overwhelm her self-control, and she had to fight with every ounce of willpower not to react.

"Now, you'll feel a little pop," Dr. Maerwynn said.

Those fingers dug under her face. Searing heat burned down along her jaw and Sarah lost control.

She screamed.

Her face came free with a pop.

The scream trailed off to a whisper while the pain faded, as did all sensory input. She couldn't feel anything, not even the sleeplike numbness of the doll's body. Her face was still covered so she couldn't see anything. She didn't seem to be breathing. That should have terrified her, but she felt no lack of air. Her mind was drawn to the one sense that seemed greatly magnified. Hearing.

Dr. Maerwynn's breathing thundered like a bellows, while the swish of cloth sounded like the rush of a hurricane as the doctor lifted her face free and turned toward the gurney. Then there was another flash of heat, and feeling rushed back, nearly overwhelming her.

Again she felt muscles, skin, hair. It was like every part of the body she now owned wanted to connect with her mind at the same time.

The cloth snapped free of her face and vision returned. Dr. Maerwynn leaned forward, watching her closely. "Take it easy. The transfer is a little abrupt without the tranquilizer."

Sarah sat upright in one convulsive move. Her muscles quivered and her entire body shivered with goose bumps.

"What did you do?" She couldn't let Dr. Maerwynn know that she knew.

"We haven't quite perfected the transfer from the dolls yet. We're working on it."

Sarah managed a weak smile and was grateful when Dr. Maerwynn turned back to Jill. Sarah looked down at her new body to see what they'd given her.

It wasn't old. She let out a sigh of relief. Then she paused, a glimmer of hope making it hard to breathe.

The body looked familiar.

Sarah slipped off the gurney and stepped to the full-length mirror. The body wore only undergarments. It was young, with graceful curves. It felt fit and healthy.

She stared in the mirror with wonder. It looked like her own. She examined it closely, running hands down her flanks, feeling her face and hair.

She closed her eyes and breathed deep.

It was a very close match, but it wasn't her body. The differences were subtle, but she could feel as much as see them. She opened her eyes again and considered her reflection. She brought her hands in front of her face and peeked between her fingers.

Then it hit her. She knew this body.

The convict.

Sarah sagged against the gurney, trying to keep the horror from her face. She was wearing a stolen body while the convict was locked away in that tiny coffin.

Would they ever let her out?

"How do you like it?" Dr. Maerwynn asked. She strode over to Sarah and gave her an appraising look.

"It's very nice," Sarah managed to say.

Dr. Maerwynn frowned. "You have no idea how hard it was to find such a close match. I don't think you're worth all the trouble, but Mr. Fleischer insisted." She leaned closer and said, "I suggest you keep that in mind when you meet with him."

"I will."

"Good. Now go. Don't keep him waiting."

Sarah slipped into the simple blue sun dress laid out for her. It looked very good on her new body. Jill, who still lay on the counter as a doll, gave her a tiny thumb's up signal. Without a word, she left the room and headed for Mr. Fleischer's office.

She barely made it to the first restroom before vomiting noisily into the toilet. Then she huddled against the cool porcelain while shudders wracked her frame.

It took several minutes to regain her composure and clean herself off. Periodic spasms still rippled through her as her body reacted to the terror bubbling in her mind.

Forcing calm on her face, Sarah entered the elevator and rode it up to the top floor. On the way up, she decided how she would handle Mr. Fleischer.

CHAPTER 15

W ell, Sarah, have you considered our proposal?"
Mr. Fleischer smiled, clearly confident of
victory, while Lawyer Guy opened his briefcase.

"I have," she said, pleased that she managed to keep her voice steady and sounding calm, despite her racing heartbeat.

Mr. Fleischer nodded toward her new body. "Once you sign the document, we'll sign over permanent ownership of your new body to you. You'll hardly know anything is different."

"It is a very close match, sir."

"Very good. You've made a wise choice, Sarah."

Lawyer Guy pulled the sheaf of papers from his briefcase, but before he could pass them across to her, Sarah held up a hand. Her fingers trembled only a little as she made her play.

"Sir, I have one condition." Mr. Fleischer's smile faded a little. "Before I sign, I want to meet the renter in person."

"Sarah, you know our policy."

"I know, sir, but I need to look her in the eye and know she'll take good care of it." She paused and looked down at her hands. She hoped that made her look submissive, but really she couldn't risk him seeing her fury blazing in her eyes. Forcing herself to speak softly she added, "I want a moment to say good-bye."

She looked up and met Mr. Fleischer's gaze, hoping her attempt at innocent honesty was working.

"You're just making it harder on yourself."

"It's a reasonable request. I'm a sentimental girl. Please."

Mr. Fleischer waved a hand dismissively. "Fine." Then he leaned forward, "But no second thoughts. No hysterics."

"Of course not. I just want a few minutes alone with her, with my old body."

"Ten minutes."

"That should be enough."

To Lawyer Guy he said, "Set it up. I want this wrapped up by tomorrow."

"Sir, can I ask how you found someone who looked so much like me in so short a time who was willing to sign over permanent corporal possession to me?"

"That is not your concern."

"She has agreed to sign the body over to me, right?"

"Of course," Mr. Fleischer lied with a straight face. "All the documents will be in order."

Sarah had no doubt they would be.

Mr. Fleischer reached for his phone. "Now that this is settled, please excuse me."

Sarah rose and managed to not sprint for the door.

CHAPTER 16

Sarah found Tomas in the labyrinthine depths of the transfer facility and pulled him into an empty transfer station. Doubts and fear about what she'd just agreed to made her mouth dry. She found it difficult to speak, but forced the words out.

"You wouldn't have shown me that transfer if you didn't know of a way to help me."

"You needed to know the truth, Sarah."

"Stop! Don't play games with me. I don't have time for it. You showed me, I get it, I'm in. Whatever it takes. I'll help you with whatever you're planning. Just promise me I'll get to keep my own body."

Tomas smiled. "I was hoping you'd say that, although you're moving faster than I thought you would."

"I can't afford to hesitate. They want me to sign over permanent corporal possession tomorrow."

"We don't have much time," Tomas said with a frown, but he sounded determined rather than worried. Sarah took that as a good sign.

"I arranged a private meeting with the renter to say good-bye."

Tomas smiled. "Brilliant. We can work with that."

"Will Dr. Maerwynn help us?"

"No."

"Will one of her medical assistants help?"

"No."

"Then who? You've got to have a plan to get around them, right? They're not the only people who can do a transfer?"

"No, they are not."

"Then who?"

Tomas sighed. "I'm going to have to ask you to trust me on that part."

"You're kidding."

"No. Trust me on this, and we'll get your body. I promise."

Sarah took a deep breath. That was not exactly reassuring, but what choice did she really have? "What do we do?"

"You need to go talk with Jill."

"Hold on, Jill won't help us. You've got to know that."

"She will."

"I doubt it. She's only motivated by money."

"She'll get it. But you're wrong—there's one thing that'll motivate her more."

"Like what?"

"Like learning about the real health risks tied to transfers."

That surprised Sarah. "What kind of health risks?"

"The risks are minimal to the renters, but for donors—you who transfer many times—the risks are very real."

"Like what?" Sarah demanded. She shouldn't be surprised that there were even more secrets, but she wasn't sure how many more she could handle.

"You've already seen the early stages, Sarah. You think that weird memory of that beach house in the Caymans was a fluke?"

"Yes," she said without conviction. That memory had felt completely real.

"Or Jill's comment about shopping for birthday cards for grandkids?"

"That was pretty weird," she admitted.

"It's more than weird. It's dangerous. That so-called nervous breakdown of Irina's was the corporation's way of hiding the transfer sickness."

"What happened to her?" Sarah asked, but she was starting to think maybe she didn't want to know.

"Too many face leaps. Each transfer uses up a little of a soul's power. After too many, the soul becomes too weak to maintain its integrity, and wisps of lingering identity from the bodies they inhabit begin to seep in to fill in the cracks. With enough transfers, it drives people insane."

"That's horrible." Sarah hadn't thought things could get any worse. She wanted to ask Tomas what else he was keeping from her, but didn't dare.

"The machinery they use in the transfers is experimental. It's designed to filter brainwaves and block mental dissipation or psychic bleed. It helps, but it's not perfect."

"So eventually we'll all end up like Irina?"

"Or worse. Think of the worst psychopaths in world history. A large percentage of them were suffering from leap insanity. It's not a new problem."

"Tomas, I can't process this right now. It's too crazy."

"Then just believe me when I say the situation is a lot more dangerous than you understand. I'll give you some internal documentation from Dr. Maerwynn herself for Jill to read. That'll convince her to help."

Sarah nodded. That would work, and maybe Jill would understand enough to escape Alterego before it destroyed her.

"Why don't you just explain it to her?"

Tomas smiled. "I have to write a letter."

CHAPTER 17

W alter, have you seen this?" Gladys sat up in the padded pool chair where she'd been lounging, and twisted the laptop so Walter could take a look at the screen. He sat up in his own chair and removed his sunglasses. His muscles rippled across his chest as he shifted toward her.

"What is it, dear? I hope it's not a new model. I'm very happy with the ones we've got."

"No, it's an email from Alterego. It's stamped classified, internal eyes only."

Walter chuckled. "Someone's going to get fired." He leaned forward, interested. "Did they leak any juicy secrets?"

Gladys met his gaze, her expression worried. "It says there are serious health risks for renters that they need to conceal."

"What?"

Walter took the proffered laptop and scanned the email. Emblazoned across the top in bold, red letters was the warning, "Classified Material. Internal Eyes Only." The email consisted of several paragraphs of highly technical gibberish that Walter could not understand. His eyes were drawn to the highlighted text at the bottom.

The health risks are irrefutable. Seventy-five percent of donors are likely to experience at least one symptom, and at least fifty percent may experience life-threatening side-effects.

We recommend immediate cancellation of all leases. If the truth of these risks becomes public, the corporation would face massive lawsuits. Losses would be catastrophic and leave the future of Alterego in doubt. Marketing is working on materials to disseminate false information to shield the company from liability.

Walter whistled and shared a fearful look with Gladys. They glanced down at their gorgeous rental bodies, and for the first time wondered if they'd made a mistake.

Walter reached for the phone. All lines at Alterego were busy and he waited impatiently on hold. While he waited, Gladys took the laptop back from him.

"Walter, another email."

"What does it say?"

Gladys scanned it. "It says to ignore the last email. That it was a scam sent by a disgruntled employee."

Walter hung up the phone. "Do you believe it?"

"I don't know."

In Alterego's corporate facility, an elderly woman waiting for her next rental body called over a pretty young staff member in a white lab coat.

"Excuse me, miss." She held up her smartphone. "Did you see the email that just went out from the corporation?"

"Yes, ma'am," the young woman said with a serious expression. "We're all very concerned."

"Really? What about the second email that said those health risks were all a lie?"

Several other renters seated nearby leaned closer to listen.

"Oh, of course." The woman smiled reassuringly, but her eyes looked worried. "Sorry, my mistake. I meant that we're all concerned . . . about who would do such a terrible thing."

"So, there are no health risks?"

The young woman looked around nervously, "Will you excuse me? I just remembered I'm late for an appointment."

Without waiting for a reply, she all but ran from the room.

"She's the worst liar I've ever seen," said an old man seated nearby. "I was a trial lawyer and I can spot 'em a mile away."

"So you think they're trying to cover it up?"

The man nodded and pulled out his phone, "I'm calling my son's law firm. They'll have papers filed within the hour demanding full disclosure."

Word spread quickly across the waiting room. Some of the renters converged on the attendant seated at the nearby help desk and peppered him with questions. The more he denied knowledge of any health risks, the angrier they became.

Within ten minutes, a dozen emails were posted on Alterego's renter-only mail server warning everyone of the danger.

Within half an hour, every one of those emails were removed as spam by the server administrator.

That was when the panic really started.

Sarah, still dressed in a white lab coat, peeked through a window at the growing tumult in the waiting room. It was working better than she'd imagined.

Now for the hard part.

CHAPTER 18

Someone tell me who wrote that email!"

Mr. Fleischer paced angrily in his office near the fireplace in front of his senior staff who sat anxiously in the sofas and padded chairs.

"We don't know for sure," the CIO said, mopping his expansive forehead with a cloth. "It originated from within the corporation, but the account was false. There is no Office of Internal Risk Assessment."

Mr. Fleischer rounded on the man. "It's been almost twenty-four hours. The situation is spiraling out of control. I need to know!"

"We're working on it, sir. The perpetrator somehow disabled our network security during the time period in question so we have little information."

"Have you determined who authorized the deletion of those renter emails? That was the stupidest thing I've ever seen. It just confirmed in everyone's minds that we're trying to cover something up."

The CIO shook his head. "We believe this might be the work of the same person who sent the original email. The server that audits all access to the mail accounts crashed and we haven't been able to bring it back online yet."

Mr. Fleischer paced away, hands clenched into fists. "I've got lawsuits demanding full disclosure being filed in five states."

Lawyer Guy interrupted. "We can stall those for a while."

"I don't want them stalled!" Mr. Fleischer roared. "We can't have this kind of attention. We can't hold up to a full-blown audit."

The Chief Publicist said, "There are three news crews parked outside, interviewing everyone they can get their hands on."

"When did this happen?"

"Just before we convened."

The head of security, a beefy ex-military officer said, "I could have my boys throw them out."

"No, that would only make things worse."

The Chief Publicist said, "The best way to subdue this panic and settle things down is to present a unified message." She handed out files to everyone. "My office has already prepared statements for your review. Once approved, I'll deal with the news media. We've recalled all staff members to assist with fielding phone calls and reassuring worried renters."

"Good, that will help." Mr. Fleischer rounded on the CIO and the head of security. "You two need to track down whoever is responsible. I want their heads."

Dr. Maerwynn spoke for the first time. "My assistants are working overtime restoring renters who have demanded early termination of their leases. At this point, we're looking at probably thirty percent return rate."

Mr. Fleischer ran a hand across his face. "Thirty percent?"

"It could be worse."

"Anything else." When no one spoke up, Mr. Fleischer dismissed them. Dr. Maerwynn lingered behind after the others left.

"This is a delicate situation, Michael."

"I know. We can handle it."

"Make sure you do. I can't afford to have this operation endangered."

"I'll manage my end. Don't worry."

Mr. Fleischer's secretary stuck her head in the office. "Sir, Marilyn is here."

"Send her in."

"Are you still moving forward with the permanent corporal transfer?" Dr. Maerwynn asked. "I thought we agreed to postpone it."

He shrugged. "She insisted. Besides, we need some positive press right now."

Marilyn entered the office, dressed in a conservative but attractive business suit. Mr. Fleischer took her hand. "You look fantastic."

"Thank you, Mr. Fleischer," she said with a smile. "Now where is this wonderful young woman I am to meet?"

Mr. Fleischer led her down one floor to a small conference room. He frowned when he found it empty. "Please wait here, Marilyn. Sarah will be here shortly."

He left and strode quickly down the hall.

As soon as Mr. Fleischer turned the far corner, Sarah emerged from her hiding place in the next office. She went to the conference room and after taking a deep, steadying breath, pushed open the door. The woman standing across the room, dressed in a ladies' business suit, was wearing Sarah's body.

The sight of it made Sarah want to laugh and cry at the same time. It was such a relief to see herself looking so good, but she wanted to claw out the eyes of that interloper.

Sarah forced calm. *Follow the plan, and everything will be fine.*

"You must be Sarah," the woman said.

"Yes, I am."

"I am so pleased to meet you. My name is Marilyn."

Sarah took the extended hand and fought the freaky feeling that she was living an Alfred Hitchcock episode.

Marilyn beamed. Her face looked nice. It fit Sarah's body surprisingly well. Marilyn gave a girlish laugh and said, "Look at us. We could almost be sisters."

Sarah smiled.

"You have no idea how grateful I am that you accepted my offer."

Before Sarah could find words to reply, the conference room door opened. Jill, dressed in lab whites over an athletic body known as 'Soccer Star,' pushed a gurney inside.

"What's this?" Marilyn asked with a frown.

"Don't worry," Jill said in her most professional voice. "We need to take some vitals prior to the final transfer sign-off. Mr. Fleischer felt it would be more convenient to do it here."

"That was thoughtful of him." Marilyn lay back on the gurney. To Sarah she added, "My dear, you've given me the most wonderful gift anyone could receive."

"It was nothing," she lied, struggling to maintain the neutral mask covering her nervousness.

"Oh, but it is! People have been searching for the fountain of youth forever. Today, you are giving it to me."

Jill jabbed a tranquilizer needle into Marilyn's arm and injected the chemical in a single, fluid motion.

"What was that for?" Marilyn exclaimed.

Jill smiled down at her. "We're just going to . . ." Marilyn's eyes closed before she finished. Jill looked Marilyn over and said, "Kind of freaky, isn't it?"

"You have no idea." Sarah stared at the sleeping woman for a moment, fighting a flash of guilt. Pushing the feeling aside, she maneuvered the gurney toward the door. "Come on. We have to hurry."

Jill pulled a large umbrella from under the gurney and shook it open.

"Ready."

Mr. Fleischer returned to his office and told his secretary to track down Sarah. With everything else going wrong, he could not afford to have that woman causing trouble.

After a few minutes, his secretary reported, "Sir, no one seems to know where Sarah is."

Mr. Fleischer rose to his feet. "Curse that girl." He strode from the office, but before he could reach the elevator, it opened and the auditor, still wearing 'Conan' stepped out.

Even his weak-faced frown looked intimidating on that body. He said, "Mr. Fleischer, we need to talk."

"Please wait in my office. I'll only be a few minutes."

The auditor held out a powerful arm to bar the way. "I am sorry, sir, but this cannot wait. My superiors want a report within the hour. I have some questions that need answering immediately."

Mr. Fleischer forced a smile. "Of course. Please join me."

To his secretary he said, "See to it that someone keeps an eye on Marilyn until Sarah arrives."

"Yes, sir."

It took ten minutes to find someone available to handle the low priority assignment of baby-sitting a renter who was not screaming about lawsuits. A junior staffer showed up at the conference room only to find it empty.

CHAPTER 19

M r. Fleischer was answering a mind-numbing list of questions from the auditor when his secretary peeked into the office. "Excuse me, sir. Which office is Marilyn waiting in?"

"The Napoleon room."

She frowned. "Sir, no one is in that room."

At that moment, the lights flickered and went out.

Then the fire alarm began to wail.

The sprinklers kicked on three seconds later.

CHAPTER 20

Pandemonium reigned at Alterego.

Renters exited the building, drenched from the fire suppressant system, while staff scrambled to wheel out all the renters' bodies. They assembled the gurneys of carefully-covered bodies, each capped with an opaque life support unit, in a distant corner of one parking lot. They roped off the area and posted a dozen staffers to keep curious media and renters at bay.

Ecstatic news crews started live feeds and hunted for stories, and more than one tried to get into the building. Police and fire trucks responded within moments, the wailing of their sirens adding to the din and confusion.

Inside the main building, Mr. Fleischer arrived in the central control room in a towering fury, his hand-crafted suit ruined.

"What the devil is going on here." he roared. Staffers cringed away from his fury.

The head of security saluted out of habit, "Sir, we had a massive power failure and five simultaneous fire sensor alerts."

"Where's the fire?"

The man frowned. "That's the thing, sir. We haven't found any. It looks like the sensors all malfunctioned."

"All of them? At the same time?"

"It appears so."

"You idiot! It's that saboteur. He's struck again."

"I considered that, sir, but the cameras show the vault is secure and I have men posted at the entry points to the main offices. Nothing of value is vulnerable."

Mr. Fleischer pointed to the wall of monitors that cycled through the multitude of security cameras installed in and around the facility. "Show me the outside." A technician typed a couple of keys, and half a dozen monitors shifted to views of the chaos outside.

"That's what he's after. He's causing a panic."

The fire alarm siren stopped wailing and Mr. Fleischer blew out a breath. "About time." He surveyed the views from the various cameras, "Get me Dr. Maerwynn. We need to get a handle on this situation."

Five minutes later, as he met with Dr. Maerwynn and the representatives of the local fire and police departments, a staffer handed him a printout. "Sir, all visitors accounted for but one."

"Not bad," a police officer said. "With everyone coming and going, I'm impressed you can keep such a close count."

Mr. Fleischer nodded toward the head of security. "We run a tight ship here. The missing person probably left during the confusion. We'll check the halls to verify everyone is safe."

"Yes, sir," the security chief said, looking pleased.

"Send the all-clear, and start wheeling those renters back into their suites."

The staffer nodded and turned to leave, but paused. "Oh, the missing visitor's name is Marilyn."

Mr. Fleischer's face drained of color. "What did you say?"

"Marilyn, sir."

He shared a look with Dr. Maerwynn and then turned to the chief of security. "Please show these gentlemen around the facility so they can confirm all is well."

"Yes, sir."

As soon as the door closed behind them, Mr. Fleischer turned to Dr. Maerwynn. "Sarah didn't meet us at the conference room, but when we went back to get Marilyn, she was already gone."

Dr. Maerwynn frowned. "You think she's done something rash?"

"Possibly."

"This could be a disaster."

Mr. Fleischer turned to the security staffers. "Seal the outer gates. No one goes in or out of this facility without I.D. verification. Search every vehicle. Sarah must be found."

One staffer pointed at the cluster of emergency vehicles. "Sir, we can't search those. We'll need to tell the police."

"No, just verify identities of everyone else who tries to leave."

The security staffers scrambled to make calls on phones and radios. Dr. Maerwynn pulled Mr. Fleischer aside to converse quietly.

"She must know she can't restore herself alone. Only I or my assistants can do it."

"Does she really know that?"

Dr. Maerwynn frowned. "Perhaps not."

Mr. Fleischer tapped one of the security staffers, "You, scan through all the cameras in the transfer lab. See if anyone is moving around down there."

"Yes, sir."

Dr. Maerwynn moved up beside him as images started flashing past. "We're overlooking something here, Michael. I can feel it."

CHAPTER 21

Sarah peeked around a corner. The hall ran clear and empty to a large room with an unmanned security desk. Behind the desk loomed the gigantic steel door of the closed vault, with its massive wheel that spun the many locking pins.

"Come on. Coast is clear."

She pulled the gurney around the corner while Jill pushed from behind. Jull had dropped the huge umbrella as soon as the sprinklers stopped. It had kept her and the sleeping Marilyn mostly dry.

Sarah hadn't been so lucky. The umbrella was big, but not that big. Her soaked clothing clung to her figure, and her wet hair was plastered to her head. She probably looked like a drowned puppy. She wiped water out of her face and slowed as they approached the security desk.

"Tomas." she called softly.

He popped up from behind the desk, and Sarah jumped with a cry of surprise. "Don't do that!"

"Sorry. Just finishing disabling the vault door alarm." He paused, eyes drawn to her sodden, clinging clothing. He looked away quickly, and actually started to blush.

That was sweet, and surprising. He saw mostly naked bodies all the time. Although she wasn't wearing her own body, Sarah didn't like people ogling her, and she appreciated the fact that he didn't keep staring. Most men would.

Tomas instead typed a few keys on the keyboard hidden behind the desk. "We should be good to go."

"I hope you're right," Sarah said as she pulled at her shirt to loosen its clinging hold on her skin.

"Trust me."

Tomas strode to the vault, spun the large wheel to release the locks, and hauled the massive door open. It swung easily on silent hinges, despite its enormous weight. He stepped through the eight foot wide door and flicked on an interior light.

"I thought the power was out," Sarah said as she followed.

"The vault's on an independent grid."

Tomas led the way inside. Despite her anxiety, Sarah couldn't help but look around with wonder at the huge space. Racks of what looked like safety deposit boxes rose over fifteen feet into the air and stretched back into the darkness beyond the lights.

Sarah stared at the boxes in horror. Could there really be people in all of them, faces removed, locked away in those tiny coffins?

Jill looked around and frowned. "I thought there were holding cells in here. What's with the bank stacks?"

"The holding cells are back there," Tomas said, pointing to the left, toward an area concealed by deep shadows.

"Creepy."

Sarah pulled the gurney farther into the room. "What do we do now?"

Tomas ran to a single workstation and began to type quickly. After a moment he smiled and blew out a breath, looking relieved. "Got her."

"Her?"

"I'll be right back."

Without waiting for a reply, he dashed off into the darkness of the vault stacks. His voice called back to them. "There are three bodies in the closest transfer station. Wheel them in here. Then bring me one more empty gurney. Hurry."

CHAPTER 22

T here." Dr. Maerwynn pointed toward one of
the monitors.

On the screen, Sarah and another white-
coated person whose back was turned to the camera were pushing an empty gurney down a hall.

"Where's Marilyn?" Mr. Fleischer asked.

"Follow them," Dr. Maerwynn commanded.

The staffer typed a command, and other monitors flashed to different views of the transfer lab.
They watched the two women push the empty gurney down a couple of corridors.

Then they rounded a corner and disappeared
from view.

"Where are they?" Mr. Fleischer demanded.

The staffer frowned and pointed at the monitor
right in front of him that showed the empty vault
antechamber. "They should be right there, sir."

"They've tampered with the camera," Dr. Maerwynn hissed. "They're in the vault."

"What are they doing there?" Mr. Fleischer asked.

Dr. Maerwynn suddenly gasped. "Come on! We have to get down there immediately." Without waiting for a reply, she yanked out her phone and barked, "Call Mai Luan." Even as the phone processed the voice command, she bolted from the room.

Mr. Fleischer pointed at three of the security staffers in the room. "You three. Come with me."

"But sir . . ." one of them protested.

"Now, or you're fired."

Together, they sprinted toward the vault.

CHAPTER 23

Tomas returned just as Sarah and Jill pushed the empty gurney into the vault beside the one that held the sleeping Marilyn. He placed one of the tiny face coffins on the floor next to the gurney.

Sarah blew out a breath. "We had to check four transfer stations before we found this."

"Sorry. Should have warned you about that." Tomas nodded toward the male bodies they'd wheeled in earlier. "Come on, help me push these over to the holding cells and remove the life support units."

"Why?"

"Insurance."

They returned to the gurney with the sleeping Marilyn a few minutes later and Tomas told Jill to lie down.

Jill obeyed but looked at the box questioningly. "What's in there?"

Tomas shared a look with Sarah. "Best you don't know. I don't think you're ready for it."

"You told me about the real health risks, so why not this?"

"You want to be able to sleep at night?"

Jill shrugged. "Fine, be that way. Just make sure I get the bonus you promised."

Tomas pulled a syringe from his pocket and slipped the tip smoothly into Jill's arm. "I promise."

As the fast-acting drug dragged Jill down to unconsciousness, Sarah felt a pang of guilt. "Will she really get a bonus?"

"Hopefully. At the least she'll keep her sanity."

Sarah stroked Jill's sleeping cheek. "She'll be fine. She's the number one donor."

Tomas flipped open the lid of the little coffin and extracted a face. Unlike the one Sarah had seen earlier, this one was small, the size of a doll's face. It was dark, with only a little gray mist floating beneath it.

It looked dead.

Sarah saw again in her mind the shimmering mask of the other extracted face, with its bright rainbow mist, and wondered at the difference.

Tomas inspected the face carefully and whispered. "Eirene, can you hear me?"

He placed the face next to his ear and waited. After a moment he grinned and blew out a relieved sigh. Sarah hadn't heard anything.

"You've been locked away a long time . . . No . . . Gregorios sent me."

Sarah watched the one-sided conversation with a frown until she noticed the face's lips twitch a little. Maybe it was still alive after all.

Reality had become too bizarre, but she forced herself not to question it. She'd witnessed the face transfers earlier, and there was no going back.

Tomas spoke again. "We have a host for you. She's unconscious and willing, but you'll have to manage the full transfer. Can you do it?"

This time Sarah heard the tiniest whisper.

"*Yes.*"

"There's not much time."

Tomas positioned the face over Jill's head and lowered it down until it almost touched. The thin, gray streamers floating beneath the face caressed Jill's skin.

As Sarah watched, the streamers began to shift to light gray, and then to white. More streamers appeared, coiling down from under the face, and began rippling into different colors. The face itself began to slowly expand and brighten until it more closely resembled the shimmering mask Sarah had seen before.

The motion of the rainbow streamers changed. They flowed over Jill's face with purpose, no longer idly caressing, and concentrated around the boundary of her jaw. All at once, they tightened. The mask-like face began to glow with a bright purple light, and the muscles along Tomas' arms and shoulders flexed as he leaned back, helping pull against Jill's face.

Although Sarah knew it was necessary, she had to fight to remain still, a silent witness to the monstrous process. Part of her wanted to leap forward and slap the living relic away from her friend.

She could not. It was her only hope for her own salvation.

Within seconds, Jill's peacefully sleeping face began to lift from the skull with that disgusting, wet sucking sound. Sarah grimaced and covered her ears as skin slid away and Jill's face came free with a loud pop. Tomas lifted it high, a shimmering mask with rainbow streamers floating beneath it.

Was that her soul?

Tomas placed the other face over the blank skull and it sank into place, with flesh flowing up and over it to bind it to the body. The face shook like Jell-O in the hands of a running child as it united with the body. He let go and, as the shaking settled over the next couple of seconds, he carefully deposited Jill's face into the tiny coffin.

"Don't you dare close her in," Sarah snapped. The thought of her friend being locked away filled her with horror.

"I won't. Now get over here quick and take her legs."

Sara moved to obey while Tomas leaned his weight over the body's upper torso, pinning the arms down against the gurney.

"What's going on?" Sarah asked.

The body convulsed hard, every limb whipping up into the air like it had been hit with a massive electric shock. Sarah hadn't been holding tight enough, and she was knocked back several steps.

"Help me," Tomas called as he fought to restrain the wildly thrashing body.

Sarah rushed back toward the gurney, only to get kicked in the chest by one flailing leg and dumped back onto the floor.

"Hurry," Tomas called.

Sarah gave him a dirty look, but threw herself back to her feet and tackled the lower half of the convulsing woman. As she held on with all her strength, she shouted, "Why is she doing this?"

"She's been unincorporated a long time. It's a shock uniting with a new system after so long."

Sarah recalled the rush of sensation when she'd been transferred from the doll. She'd lost her sense of touch and smell only for seconds, and the experience had almost overwhelmed her when it all came roaring back. How would it have felt if she'd been bereft of those senses for . . . how long?

The two of them fought to hold the body down for half a minute before the convulsing slowed. Tomas straightened, wiped sweat from his face, and gingerly fingered a bruise already darkening under one eye where the thrashing head had connected.

The woman lay quiet, breathing hard, staring unblinking up toward the ceiling. Her face looked mature, strong, and very striking. It fit the 'Soccer Star' body well.

"Who is she?" Sarah asked in a whisper.

The woman sat up smoothly. She smiled and extended one hand in a jerky motion. "I am Eirene. Pleasure to meet you." She spoke with an archaic British accent.

Sarah took the proffered hand. "I'm Sarah."

"That body looks good on you."

"Thanks." How could the woman know?

Eirene turned to Tomas. "Interesting choice of suit. Glad you're here. What's the situation?"

Tomas gestured at the vault around them. "We're in enemy territory. We need to move fast."

Eirene swung her legs off the gurney. "Very well. Lead the way."

Sarah held up a hand. "Hold on a minute. What about me?"

Tomas explained to Eirene. "I promised you'd return her to her own body after we freed you." He nodded toward the sleeping Marilyn.

Eirene rose to her feet and surveyed her new body for a moment, and then took a tentative step. "Very well."

Tomas' phone beeped three times loudly. He glanced at the partially open vault door. "We've got company."

He ran to the vault door and peeked through, and then retreated rapidly to them. "There's a crowd out there, including Mr. Fleischer and Dr. Maerwynn."

Eirene hissed like an angry cat, "Maer. She'll regret interfering with me today."

"What do we do?" Sarah asked.

"They haven't seen any of us yet." Tomas pulled a long knife from one deep pocket and handed it to Sarah. "You need to hold them off for a few minutes."

Sarah looked at the knife fearfully. "I can't fight them."

Tomas smiled. "You won't have to."

CHAPTER 24

D r. Maerwynn paused outside of the vault behind Mr. Fleischer. The door stood partially ajar and lights glowed from within, but they could not see inside without stepping to the entrance.

Mai Luan whispered from close behind her, "They can't take any souls out of the vault."

Dr. Maerwynn waved her to silence. Mr. Fleischer was a useful puppet, but knew nothing of the truth behind their work in the vault.

Mr. Fleischer motioned the guards ahead. At the entrance they paused. "Sir, you'll want to see this."

Dr. Maerwynn followed him to the threshold, where she hesitated, just outside the door. Only rarely did she enter the vault, leaving it to Mai Luan and her arcane Cui Dashi purposes. She always felt a hint of fear crossing the threshold into Mai Luan's domain, although she'd never allow the other woman to sense her discomfort.

Sarah stood twenty feet inside the vault at the head of a gurney, with a long knife held to the sleeping Marilyn's throat.

"Stop right there or she dies," Sarah said in a shaky voice.

Dr. Maerwynn stepped across the threshold, focusing on her anger at Sarah rather than the thought of the runes carved into the lintels of the vault doorway. She would have to reprimand Mr. Fleischer for pressing ahead with the full corporal transfer against her better judgment. The risk to their operation was far too great for the hoped-for return.

"You won't kill her. You're not the suicidal type."

"Better that my body die with her than let her steal it."

"Sarah, you're not helping matters," Mr. Fleischer said from close beside Dr. Maerwynn. "Put the knife down and we'll talk."

Sarah shook her head and pointed the knife at him. "Talking with you is useless. You don't listen. You won't accept any terms but your own." She glared at him. "I won't sign that contract."

"What do you want?" Dr. Maerwynn asked, taking a step forward. Sarah was right about Mr. Fleischer being a blockhead, but the foolish woman could ruin everything.

"I want my body back. I want out of this place."

"You'll release Marilyn if we agree?"

"Yes."

Dr. Maerwynn shared a glance with Mr. Fleischer. He grimaced and nodded. It would have to be done.

"Very well, Sarah. After we complete the transfer, your employment will be terminated."

"Fine by me."

She stepped closer. "Then put down the knife and we'll return to one of the transfer stations."

"No, I don't trust you."

"Then how can we proceed?"

Sarah glanced around uncertainly, and Dr. Maerwynn took another step forward. "Sarah, in order to meet your demands we need to go to a transfer station. You'll have to trust me."

Sarah hesitated and then nodded.

Dr. Maerwynn took another step forward. Good, the foolish girl would cooperate. Another few steps and she could take possession of the knife. No one had stood up to Maerwynn so effectively in decades. Usually she would appreciate the challenge, but the timing was far too inconvenient.

Another few seconds and she would introduce Sarah to tortures only recently re-discovered by their archaeological teams. She would be privileged to die by Nepthys' ancient preferred method.

Sarah moved the knife away from Marilyn as Dr. Maerwynn took another step forward. Only five steps to go.

That was when she noticed the face coffin lying open on the floor beside the gurney. Who had been stored there? How would Sarah even know to search the coffins?

Sarah watched Dr. Maerwynn approaching with barely concealed panic.

It's working.

Where's Tomas?

Now, for the dangerous part.

Sarah held up her smartphone. "One other thing. I've taken dozens of photos of the vault, the face coffins, and their contents. I've transmitted those photos to an acquaintance. If they don't hear from me within the hour, they'll give it all to five major news organizations, as well as to the congressional oversight committee investigating Alterego."

Sarah raised her phone high and smashed it against the floor as hard as she could. Dr. Maerwynn lunged forward, one hand outstretched as if to catch it.

It shattered into half a hundred pieces.

"You fool!" Dr. Maerwynn shrieked.

Sarah smiled. "Now you can't trace those messages." Fighting to look calm, Sarah dropped the knife, "Now I'm ready for the transfer."

Everything was in place. She had Dr. Maerwynn right where she wanted her. It was going to work!

Dr. Maerwynn approached, clearly enraged. She scooped up the knife and stalked toward Sarah, murder in her eyes.

Uh oh. That wasn't part of the plan.

Sarah back-pedaled, "Just do what I ask and the photos won't be published."

"Too late for that," Dr. Maerwynn snarled, still advancing.

Mr. Fleischer rushed forward, followed by his goons. "Stop! Don't hurt her. We need those photos."

"We'll deal with the photos later," Dr. Maerwynn growled. "Sarah, you should have taken the deal you were offered. You've meddled in things you cannot comprehend."

She raised the knife. "Deadly things."

Sarah realized she'd underestimated the woman, so she turned and ran, shouting for help. Dr. Maerwynn gave chase, trailed by the others.

In that moment shadowy forms, led by Eirene, rushed out from the dim stacks. Eirene bellowed a long, continuous shout that sounded like an ancient battle-cry. It sent shivers rippling down Sarah's arms.

"Maerwynn!"

Dr. Maerwynn gasped, dropped the knife, and fled toward the exit. Eirene sprinted after her and, despite only having transferred to a new body moments earlier, wearing 'Soccer Star,' she far outpaced the fleeing doctor.

Behind her, Tomas led three burly men in a charge out of the shadows. Sarah blinked in surprise. They wore the three bodies she and Jill had wheeled into the vault earlier, but she didn't recognize the faces. Tomas must have pulled convicts out of the storage area. They looked angry, more than ready to fight after being incarcerated for however long in the spooky vault.

Close to Marilyn's gurney, Mr. Fleischer shouted to his guards, "Take them down!"

Then he turned and ran for the exit.

One of the guards produced a taser and shot the nearest convict in the torso. The electric shock jolted the man right off his feet. He shouted a garbled cry as he hit the floor and flopped there like a fish.

The second convict reached the taser-wielding guard and, with a snarl, smashed a fist into his face, crumpling the guard to the ground. Lacking any other weapons, the guards and inmates closed in a flurry of punches, kicks, curses and cries of pain.

Tomas hurtled past them, a look of cold fury on his face. In that moment he looked nothing like the pleasant medical tech Sarah knew. Tomas crash-tackled Mr. Fleischer, and the two fell in a heap.

Tomas rolled to his feet first and kicked Mr. Fleischer in the head as he tried to rise. The blow slammed him back to the floor where he lay unmoving.

Sarah scooped up the fallen knife and returned to the gurney just as Eirene caught up with Dr. Maerwynn. The doctor spun and whipped one leg around in a roundhouse kick. Eirene bulled through the hit, her forward momentum driving her into Dr. Maerwynn. The two crashed to the floor but came to their feet instantly, kicking and punching even as they rose off the ground.

Sarah stared in amazement at the two battling women. She didn't know much about fighting, but from what she'd seen in movies, those two had to be masters. Their hands and feet blurred, so fast Sarah couldn't track the individual strikes as they punched, blocked, kicked, and jumped like over-caffeinated ninjas.

Both women took several hits but did not slow as they fought back and forth across the vault in a spectacular display of grace and acrobatics. Only by comparing Eirene's movements with Dr. Maerwynn's did

Sarah recognize the small signs that Eirene had not yet
fully mastered the new body.

She fought with amazing skill for someone all
but dead for who knew how long, but some of her
moves were a little jerky, with odd, unexpected hesi-
tations. Dr. Maerwynn ducked one unusually clumsy
blow and clobbered Eirene with a heavy punch to
the face. Eirene fell, and Dr. Maerwynn fled again
for the exit.

"Knife." Eirene called out sharply.

Sarah reacted instantly to the command in the
woman's voice, and tossed the knife.

Eirene snatched it out of the air, flipped it in
her palm, and threw it at the fleeing doctor.

With a sickening thud, the knife drove deep into
the center of Dr. Maerwynn's back. She screamed and
stumbled forward to the floor as a crimson stain began spreading across the back of her white lab coat.

Sarah's stomach lurched, and she nearly heaved
its contents across the floor. White-faced, she slumped
to her knees, but could not look away.

Eirene caught up with Dr. Maerwynn, who still
struggled weakly to crawl toward the distant exit.
Eirene yanked the knife out and rolled the wounded
doctor over, eliciting another shriek of pain.

Dr. Maerwynn spat at Eirene and clawed weakly
at her arms, but Eirene swatted her hands away. Then,

eyes and hands glowing purple, she grasped Dr. Maerwynn by the head.

With fingers blazing with purple fire, Eirene grasped Dr. Maerwynn's jaw. The doctor screamed so loud the sound reverberated back and forth through the gigantic vault, and she beat at Eirene's arms with renewed vigor.

Eirene heaved, and yanked Dr. Maerwynn's face free in a single fluid move. For a couple seconds, the long nerve clusters at the back of the eyes remained attached, as if fighting removal. Purple fire rippled across Dr. Maerwynn's face and down that connection back to her body, and the air crackled with invisible energy that raised the hair along Sarah's arms.

Eirene heaved again, and the connection snapped with a sharp crack. Dr. Maerwynn's glittering face pulled free of the body, trailing nerve clusters and rainbow mist. Her scream faded to a wail that trailed off to a helium-high whisper.

Eirene threw her head back and roared an animal cry of victory. She held the doctor's face high and stepped away from the dying body that fell in a heap at her feet.

"Bring me the face coffin," Eirene commanded.

Sarah staggered to her feet and stumbled around the gurney. She bit her lip against a fresh wave of revulsion, but forced herself to grasp the living mask of Jill's face.

She was unprepared for the chill touch of the mask. It felt as if all the heat had been sucked out of it, leaving nothing but an icy shell. It was rigid, but still gave a little at her touch. The rainbow mist floating below the face drifted up to caress Sarah's lower arm, and it thrummed with unexpected vibration. Sarah shrieked and tossed the face mask away. It clattered onto the steel bed of the gurney next to Marilyn's sleeping form.

"Careful, that's your friend you're throwing around," Eirene cautioned as she joined Sarah by the gurney and dropped Dr. Maerwynn's mask inside the little coffin.

"*Don't! Don't shut me in,*" the soft whisper drifted up to them.

How could she speak at all? She lacked vocal chords, lungs, and well, everything.

Eirene snarled, "How dare you! After what you did to me." She slammed the lid home and latched it closed.

Then she straightened her hair and regarded Jill's face where it lay on the gurney. She asked in a calm tone, "And who is this? She released her hold on this body I wear with remarkable ease."

"A friend of mine. She's had a lot of practice."

Eirene raised an eyebrow. "That is not a good thing, my dear."

Behind them, the last guard fell to a well-placed kick from one of the convicts. He and his companions lay moaning on the floor, faces bruised or bloodied, and one with an arm twisted in an unnatural angle.

"The risk of psychic contamination is mitigated by a screening machine they use in conjunction with the transfers," Tomas explained as he dragged the unconscious form of Mr. Fleischer close to the gurney. "These two young women have been repossessed hundreds of times with extremely low mental dissipation."

Eirene frowned, "So many? Even with such a machine, an untrained soul subject to so much psychic trauma would dissipate their natural defenses to an alarming degree. The risk of severe memory distortion is . . . uncharted."

Tomas shrugged. "Understood, but the procedure has proven highly effective. The ramifications are far reaching."

Eirene nodded, suddenly grave. "I must examine one of these machines."

Sarah looked from one to the other, filled with a growing frustration that she understood less than a tenth of what they'd just discussed. "Look, all I want is my body back."

"You're right, my dear. The time for other intriguing discussions must wait until we have more leisure."

Sarah nodded toward the three burly convicts, who were prowling around the fallen guards, as if debating whether or not to beat them some more. "That was fast work."

"We were motivated," Tomas said.

Eirene prodded Mr. Fleischer. "What are we going to do with him?"

Tomas smiled. "I have a plan."

CHAPTER 25

After tying up the moaning guards, Tomas retrieved another gurney for Mr. Fleischer. Then Sarah led the way toward the vault exit, pushing the gurney that held the sleeping Marilyn and the face coffin that held the dispossessed Dr. Maerwynn. Jill's unmoving mask lay near Marilyn's head.

Just before Sarah reached the vault threshold, Eirene hissed, "Sarah, stop! Heka."

"What?"

"Heka." Eirene repeated the word, her expression looking more concerned than when she'd been fighting for her life against the doctor. She pointed at the thick posts of the threshold. Only then did Sarah notice symbols carved into the steel. They looked like some kind of runes, made of a mix of hieroglyphics and Chinese.

"What is that?" She reached out to trace one that recurred often, made up of three simple marks that gave the impression of a long-eared aardvark.

Eireen snatched her hand away. "Don't touch. Heka are known by many names, but their work is not to be trifled with."

Sarah wiped her hand against her leg. "So why are we stopping? Let's get out of here."

As Tomas and the three toughs clustered close to inspect the runes, Eirene shook her head. "We cannot pass with dispossessed. I recognize a few of the runes. Bad things would happen if you tried to exit with your friend and Maerwynn as they are. Tomas, did you know of this?"

"No. It must be one of Maerwynn's assistants."

Sarah snapped her fingers and glanced back into the vault. "That's right. Mai Luan came in here with the others, but I don't see her now."

Eirene turned toward the dim expanse of the vault stacks that stretched out of sight in both directions and, as Sarah began to ask another question, raised a hand for silence. "Those runes suggest she may be extremely powerful. We're in grave danger. We must neutralize her quickly. Tomas, take the right. The rest of you stay here."

Tomas scooped up the knife from the gurney, and the two moved swiftly in opposite directions into the stacks. Sarah watched them go, torn with indecision. Part of her wanted to join them, to stay close, but she didn't want to leave Marilyn and her own body.

When they escaped the vault, she needed to ask Tomas about his involvement with Eirene. Tomas had used all sorts of skills that no normal medical technician should have. She sensed that she'd stumbled into a far greater conflict.

Did she really want to know more about it?

The three toughs waited by the door, eyeing it as if wondering if it was worth the risk of rushing through, despite the vague danger Eirene feared.

One of them gave Sarah an appraising smile, and she was grateful her clothing had mostly dried. It no longer clung so closely to her figure. The man asked, "So, what do you do for fun around here?"

"You wouldn't believe me."

He shrugged and dragged a sleeve across his bloody nose. "Right now I'd believe just about anything." He examined his arm more closely and muttered, "I don't feel like myself at all."

Another of the convicts, a thick-necked fellow, gave a startled cry and pointed at the gurney. "Hey, that mask just moved."

Sarah leaned over Jill's mask-like face as the shrunken lips twitched. A whisper-thin voice barely reached her ears. "What's happening to me?"

"It's an experimental transfer, like the dolls . . . on steroids."

"Cool."

The convicts drew further back. One of them crossed himself and made a gesture to ward against evil. Sarah had seen it once on TV.

Sarah glanced back into the stacks but both Eirene and Tomas had disappeared into the gloomy expanse. Eirene's concern about Mai Luan made Sarah deeply nervous. She'd only known Eirene a few minutes, but the woman seemed so confident, despite having been imprisoned for what sounded like a long time. If she feared Mai Luan, Sarah wanted nothing more than to escape immediately.

Then she got an idea and turned back to the convicts. "Are there other bodies back there?"

The closest one shrugged again, "Baby, right now if someone told me there was a dragon back there, I'd believe it."

"Big help." Sarah hefted the face coffin holding Dr. Maerwynn, but could not bring herself to lift Jill's dispossessed face. So instead she leaned over Jill and said, "I'll be right back."

"Where you going?" the thick-necked convict asked as she headed further into the vault.

Sarah paused to scoop up the taser dropped by the first guard, "Don't touch that face and she won't hurt you. I'll be right back."

The tough guys drew another pace away from the gurney, and Sarah hid a little smile. Their nervousness would hopefully keep them docile for a while. Trying to show more confidence than she felt, Sarah headed straight back into the dimness of the vault, hoping to find a body to bring back for Jill.

She walked twenty yards, with aluminum stacks shining dully in the dimness to either side, and fought to keep from thinking about the horrific contents in those hundreds of vault boxes.

She paused at a junction that cut through the long rows just as the unmistakable sound of a scream rippled out of the darkness to her left.

CHAPTER 26

F or a moment Sarah froze, her heart in her throat.
The darkness all around seemed to deepen, and
her breathing came faster, and seemed very loud
in the stillness. Then she heard another shout, this
one angry. It sounded like Eirene.

Without allowing time to second-guess her de-
cision, Sarah slipped left, down the narrow cross-
aisle that cut through the stacks, toward the sound.
Silence descended again upon the vault as she crept
through the shadows.

She passed four long rows of vault stacks with
no sign of life, only rows upon rows of those small
locked doors. She couldn't help but wonder if they
were all filled with imprisoned souls.

As much as she tried to ignore it, the horrifying
thought lingered in the shadows at the outer fringes
of her thoughts. Whispers of fear raised goose bumps
on her arms. What would happen to them if Eirene
failed to stop Mai Luan?

Sarah had no idea what a heka was, but the fate of any of them who failed to escape the spooky vault loomed on either side of her. If she got stuck in one of those little vault coffins, no one would ever find her. It took all her willpower to keep from turning and sprinting for the exit.

No, Eirene seemed convinced that the only way to escape was to deal with Mail Luan, so Sarah forced herself forward to the next corner. Fighting to keep her nervous breathing quiet, she peeked around the corner, and spotted Eirene.

The woman stood far down the row, and was just picking herself up off the floor. Her hair was in disarray, and she looked shaken.

Between Eirene and Sarah, standing in a glowing circle and with her back to Sarah, stood Mai Luan. The circle spanned the entire corridor between the vault stacks, glowing with a harsh, yellow light. Inside the circle, inscribed right onto the light, were a series of black runes, similar to the ones carved into the lintels of the vault door.

Mai Luan was adding more runes, and it looked like she planned to line the entire outer edge of the glowing circle with them. She drew them onto the light with her finger the same way a child would draw in the mud.

Just outside of the glowing circle, two face coffins sat against the stacks, their lids open, soft rainbow light spilling from the interiors. Movement atop one of the stacks drew Sarah's gaze. A shadow slipped along the right-hand stack above where Mai Luan worked. Then the shadow leaped off the stacks and the light of the glowing circle illuminated a face.

Tomas.

As he dove for Mai Luan, Sarah gasped, her heart in her throat as she silently urged him on. Mai Luan wasn't looking. She'd never see him coming.

It didn't matter.

Several feet above Mai Luan's head, Tomas collided with an invisible barrier and bounced sideways like a basketball. He landed hard and rolled several times before coming to a stop beside Eirene.

Mai Luan glanced up as Eirene helped Tomas climb back to his feet. "I'm insulted. Even a basic warder would shield every direction. You don't even have the sense to run, as if that would help."

The casual confidence with which she spoke scared Sarah more than even the freaky glowing circle in which the woman stood. Whatever Mai Luan was doing, she appeared convinced she could easily kill them all, no matter what they did.

With arm outstretched, Eirene approached Mai Luan, but struck the invisible barrier before she got within ten feet of the circle. The air crackled with amber sparks, and she jerked her fingers back.

When Mai Luan didn't even bother to look up from the complex runes she was drawing, Eirene growled, "You can't hope to escape."

The younger woman barked a laugh but didn't pause. She completed the rune, one that looked like an Egyptian image of the sun, surrounded by a series of Chinese characters. Shuffling left, she began the next rune, her face profile to Sarah. If she continued working around the circle, she'd spot Sarah all too soon.

Tomas pounded on the invisible barrier. "Alterego will fold, the authorities will find the vault and confiscate all your souls."

"They will find nothing," Mai Luan said. She brushed her hair back and glanced up at Tomas. "Except perhaps bits of blackened bones. Haven't you started running yet?"

When he only glared, she cocked her head to one side and added to Eirene. "You were supposed to be some great legend. I'm surprised you haven't already sacrificed your servant's soul to try to stop me."

"I don't work that way."

"Pity."

Sarah couldn't bear it any longer. Eirene and Tomas were clearly at a loss for how to penetrate whatever shielding Mai Luan had erected, and just as clearly time was about to run out. Whatever inscription Mai Luan was building upon that glowing circle would obviously prove fatal for the rest of them.

So Sarah threw the soul coffin.

Just like Tomas, it rebounded off the invisible barrier about ten feet from Mai Luan's back, a good six feet short of the nearest edge of the glowing circle. Amber sparks flashed in the dimness, and for the first time, Sarah heard the barrier crackle. The soul coffin clattered loudly against the hard floor as it bounced back to Sarah's feet.

Mai Luan glanced in her direction, startled by the light and the noise. Sarah wanted to cringe away into the shadows, but there was nowhere to hide from Mai Luan's black eyes.

"Sarah, you've just leaped into dangerous waters, without even a single soul's protection." Mai Luan smiled the way a butcher might smile at a hog about to be slaughtered.

Sarah shivered. "I just want out of here."

"Too late." Mai Luan turned back to her runes.

Eirene called from the far side of the slender woman. "Sarah, only the doctor can help."

Mai Luan huffed, "Maerwynn can't pass the wards either. Even if you haven't killed her yet, she would never help you."

Sarah glanced down at the face coffin lying at her feet, and grasped at the hint she hoped Eirene was giving her. She unsnapped the lock, opened the box, and forced herself to pick up Dr. Maerwynn's glowing face.

"Thank you, my dear," Maerwynn's whisper-thin voice drifted to her ears as the thrumming rainbow mist of her soul caressed Sarah's hand and started flowing up her arm.

Before the dangerous light could reach her face, Sarah took a quick step forward and threw the mask toward the rune circle.

Mai Luan, who had just shifted further to begin drawing the last rune needed to complete the circle, glanced up at the sound of her footstep. The mocking look fell off her lips and she gasped at the sight of the face tumbling toward her runes.

It passed through the invisible barrier with a flash of crimson light.

Mai Luan shouted with fear and lunged for the face in a dive that smeared two of the runes. She landed on a couple more, and caught Dr. Maerwynn's face just before it struck the circle of light on the floor.

She was still lying across the runes.

For half a heartbeat, nothing happened. Mai Luan looked up at Sarah and their eyes met. Sarah cringed back at the sight of pure terror in the woman's gaze.

Then the black runes blazed like Roman candles, and the entire glowing circle exploded.

CHAPTER 27

A shockwave of heat, sound, and invisible force tumbled Sarah down the aisle between high stacks of coffin vaults and drowned out her scream. She flew twenty feet, landed hard and rolled several times before sliding to a painful stop face-down on the cold floor.

Her ears rang from the blast, and all she could see was the blinding after-image of the explosion. Every inch of her body ached from the wild tumble, but amazingly she didn't think she'd broken any bones. The sharp stench of burned hair clung to her nostrils.

She lay still for a moment, savoring the coolness of the stainless-steel floor against her cheek. Then she remembered Mai Luan and forced herself to sit up with a groan.

After blinking away the lights still dancing behind her eyelids, she banged the heel of one hand against her head to try to knock the ringing out of her ears. It didn't help much.

Back at what had been Mai Luan's glowing, rune-filled circle, Sarah was shocked to see the woman stagger to her feet amid a pile of blackened rubble. The stacks on either side had buckled, the bright steel surfaces charred.

Sarah had expected to see nothing but burned remains of the slender woman, like a soldier who had jumped atop a live grenade in a movie. But somehow Mai Luan had managed to survive the blast, although her long, black hair was tumbled about her head, with chunks missing, and a few shortened ends still smoldering. She wore a grimace on her blackened face, and she hunched, as if she'd torn muscles in her back.

Just as Mai Luan managed to stand fully erect, Eirene dove through the drifting smoke that still covered the area in a thick haze, and tackled her back to the ground. The two rolled over each other, shrieking like cats, and grappling for each other's faces. Eirene's hands began to glow purple. Despite her revulsion for the face removing magic, Sarah silently urged the woman on.

Mai Luan's hands began to glow too.

The two women surged to their knees together, glowing hands locked around each other's faces and, for the first time, Eirene looked genuinely frightened.

Mai Luan grinned, "Didn't expect a cui dashi, did you?"

The purple fire ringing Mai Luan's hands spiked in intensity, and Eirene cried out in pain.

Sarah didn't know what cui dashi were, but she understood enough to know it would be bad if Mai Luan won the struggle. She rushed forward to try to help.

Mai Luan rose to her feet and easily lifted the struggling Eirene into the air. She looked stronger than she had just a moment before, as if she'd already shed the effects of the explosion.

How was it possible?

Then Tomas lunged through the smoke and plunged his knife to the hilt between Mai Luan's ribs.

Sarah skidded to a stop in shock at the brutal blow, and then stared in amazement. Instead of screaming and falling dead to the ground, Mai Luan only grunted, looking more annoyed than anything. She dropped Eirene, who scrambled away on hands and knees, and back-handed Tomas before he could twist the knife or withdraw it for another strike. The blow knocked him several feet back with blood spraying from his nose and lips.

With the dagger still stuck between her ribs, Mai Luan stalked after Eirene. "I think I'll just take your head off."

"I don't think so," Sarah snarled from behind her.

She fired the taser.

The little barbs struck Mai Luan at the base of the throat just as the slender woman turned. Finally, that surprised her. Mai Luan's body convulsed under the jolting electric current, and her startled expression was priceless. Her eyes crossed, she mumbled something incoherent, and then collapsed to the ground where she lay twitching.

Sarah rushed past the fallen woman and helped Eirene to her feet. She breathed a sigh of relief to see Tomas rise on wobbly legs not far away.

"Get . . . get back here."

Sarah spun at the sound of Mai Luan's voice, and was shocked to see the woman struggling to her knees. Her eyes still looked unfocused, but her face was locked into a snarl of rage. One hand grabbed the handle of the knife and yanked it out.

The terrifying woman groaned at the self-inflicted pain, and collapsed again as blood sprayed from the wound. But almost immediately she started trying to rise.

Tomas kicked her in the head.

She fell and he kicked her again, but she grabbed at his feet, forcing him to dance back out of reach.

Eirene called, "Come on!"

She led the way back toward the vault door at a run, with Sarah and Tomas close behind. Mai Luan's shaky voice clawed at them from the darkness.

"You cannot escape."

"We'll see about that," Eirene muttered.

When they reached the vault door, Sarah was surprised to see the three convicts still standing uneasily by the entrance. She had expected to find them already gone.

The thick-necked fellow called out, "What happened?"

"We're leaving," Eirene said curtly.

Without waiting for a reply, she scooped up Jill's face and placed it over her own. Jill's mask attached to her face, and skin flowed up to cover it, sealing it into position.

Sarah blinked a couple times in surprise, but she'd seen too much, suffered too many shocks to her system. She found that the sight of a woman wearing Jill's face over her own failed to generate more than a mild surprise.

The convicts retreated, muttering curses, but Eirene ignored them. As soon as the flesh sealed around Jill's face, Eirene led the group out of the vault. Sarah tensed with fear, but Eirene passed the threshold safely. So she pushed the gurney carrying the still-sleeping Marilyn after. With the convicts following close behind, Tomas pushed the unconscious Mr. Fleisher after Sarah, and the entire group ran for the elevators.

After only a dozen strides, Jill cried out, "What's happening? Why do I feel so strange?"

"Stop fighting me," Eirene shouted through Jill's lips as she staggered into a wall.

Sarah decided not to think about how crazy that exchange sounded.

Jill spoke again. "Tomas, did I snap? You said I'd be all right for one more transfer!"

"You're fine," Tomas assured her. "Just calm down." He gestured to two of the convicts, and they picked her up by the shoulders and resumed their run for the exit.

They reached the elevators with Jill and Eirene still arguing. It was a testament to Jill's open-mindedness that she was willing to have the conversation at all and not just start screaming, or faint. Then again, Sarah wasn't sure if Jill could make them faint, or if Eirene controlled that part of the body.

When the elevator chimed and the doors swung open, the rest of the group rushed in, but Sarah hesitated. What would happen if Mai Luan recovered enough to trigger her deadly magic while they were trapped in the elevator?

What would happen if she didn't get in?

She couldn't abandon Marilyn and her body, and she certainly couldn't carry the sleeping woman up the stairs, so she took a deep breath and pushed the gurney into the elevator. It was a tight fit, but they managed it.

While she waited impatiently for the elevator to reach the ground floor, Sarah asked, "What happened back there?"

"Your quick thinking saved our lives," Eirene said.

"Who are you?" Jill asked through the same lips.

"Take it easy," Sarah reassured her. "I'll explain everything in a bit."

Tomas squeezed Sarah's shoulder and gave her a tired smile. "You did well back there. I wasn't prepared for her to be that strong."

"How could she keep fighting, even after getting hurt so bad?"

Before he could answer, the elevator reached the ground floor and the doors opened. The group rushed out into the wide main corridor that was eerily empty. It took Sarah a moment to remember that everyone had evacuated due to the false fire alarm.

At that moment, a deep rumbling began far below, and the elevator started to rattle. The floor under their feet groaned and began to flex slowly upward.

Sarah shared a terrified look with Tomas as Eirene shouted, "Run!"

They all bolted for the exit. Sarah ran, expecting any second for the entire building to blow up, or for Mai Luan to rise through the floor like the devil incarnate. Despite additional booming noises echoing up from below, and more groaning from the floor, they reached the exit doors and fled out into the parking lot.

At the site of the unconscious people on the gurneys, emergency personnel rushed to meet them, followed by police and reporters.

Before they covered thirty feet, every window in the building behind them exploded simultaneously. Everyone dove to the ground, covering faces from flying glass. Many people screamed from terror or pain, and reporters shouted, "Tell me you got that!"

Before their cameramen could respond, the central building of the Alterego corporate facility imploded, as if sucked in by an invisible giant. A raging fireball blossomed in the center of the mass of rubble and consumed the entire devastated area.

Heat blistered their exposed skin, and everyone ran for the far end of the parking lot. The roaring of the flames drowned out all conversation, and a deadly hot wind whipped in from every direction, blowing dense clouds of black smoke over everyone.

After an impressively brief moment of surprise, firefighters scrambled to respond. Trucks that had been turning to leave wheeled around, disgorging firefighters like bees from a disturbed hive.

Everyone else retreated from the dense smoke and heat. Police struggled to maintain control, while reporters scrambled for the best positions to record the disaster. Alterego personnel either stared in shock at their shattered workplace, wept with relief that they were not trapped inside, or tried to reassure the many renters that everything would be all right.

Eirene and Tomas pulled the unconscious form of Mr. Fleisher into one of the nearby ambulances while the crew was distracted treating minor burns and smoke inhalation. The three convicts were wise enough to disappear in the confusion.

Sarah waited beside the sleeping form of Marilyn in the center of the chaos until Eirene, still wearing Jill's face, emerged from the ambulance again and motioned her around the vehicle.

"Where's Tomas?"

"He will be occupied for some time. For now, let's set you straight."

"I have so many questions. I don't even know where to start."

"I know, dear, but now is not the time. I'll explain when I can."

Jill interrupted. "After you get out of my head, psycho!"

"Actually, you're in my head."

"I want out."

"Soon, Jill. Very soon."

"Sarah, just tell her to transfer me back to the doll. That was a lot more fun."

Sarah smiled. Jill would be fine. "The TV's busted."

Jill sighed and Sarah added, "Just do what Eirene says. It's the fastest way to get out."

"Alterego is toast," Jill muttered as they turned toward the fire.

"They have great insurance."

"Good. I'd better get a huge check after all this."

CHAPTER 28

Unnoticed in the chaos of firemen fighting the huge blaze, swarms of news media, and crowds of renters demanding answers, Eirene commandeered a gurney holding one of the spare female convict bodies.

With Jill's face still fastened over her own, Eirene easily convinced the attendant the body was needed for an immediate transfer. The man seemed relieved to speak with someone who looked like they knew what was going on.

They slipped into one of the few still-standing satellite buildings that lay at the outer fringes of the Alterego complex. It stood not far from the back end of the parking lot where all the renter bodies were lined up on their gurneys. The small building housed grounds maintenance machinery and a couple of small offices.

"This will do," Eirene said with a nod, and set to clearing one office so they could fit the two gurneys inside. Then she draped a hospital sheet in one corner, as if concealing something from view. With a final nod of approval, she said, "Now, let's set you right."

With growing anticipation, Sarah changed clothes with the sleeping Marilyn. Then she helped Eirene remove the life support unit covering the head of the faceless convict they had brought along. So overwhelmed was Sarah by recent events that the sight of the smooth, faceless skin of the body did not even faze her.

Eirene popped Jill's face free, and with glowing eyes, pressed it down onto the waiting body.

After a brief moment of twitching while she settled into the new body, Jill sat up and said, "That was the freakiest time of my life. Who are you?"

"Better you not know. Now off you go. Find Mr. Fleischer. He'll need your help preparing for the return transfers."

"We can't trust him." Sarah cried.

"Never fear, my dear. Tomas is taking care of everything."

"You make less sense all the time," Jill said but, at Eirene's shooing motion, she left the building.

"Now, for you."

Sarah lay down on the empty gurney. Her entire body quivered with fear as Eirene lay fingers along her jawline.

"Try to relax," Eirene whispered soothingly.

She tried, but as the searing heat of the horrible magic rippled down her jaw, Sarah cried out and grabbed at Eirene's hands. She could not bear it, and had to get those hands off her face.

Before she could pry the woman's iron grip loose, her face pulled free and she lost connection with her arms. They flopped down to the gurney at her side as her vision shifted. Everything became flat, two-dimensional, and most color drained away until it looked like she viewed the world through an old black-and-white television.

Eirene sat her down on a nearby counter, and she couldn't help but laugh hysterically at how ridiculous it was to be looking out at the world through a shimmering face mask. She couldn't breathe, but her voice still emerged from shrunken lips, a whisper of its normal strength. She couldn't smell anything, but her ears worked exceptionally well.

Although she could not turn her head, had no head to turn, she clearly heard Eirene remove Marilyn's face and apply it to the body Sarah had just vacated. A moment later, Eirene returned Sarah to her own body and pressed her face in place.

A rush of feeling flooded her mind. Her lungs, muscles, skin, and every inch of her body clamored for attention as everything reattached in a rush. She gasped a deep breath, and laughed aloud at the wonderful feeling of *rightness.*

She was home. Everything felt right, from the weight of her hair to the tips of her toes.

"Hurry now, dear. Move along before Marilyn wakes up." Eirene helped her rise, and ushered her behind the curtain.

Only seconds later, Marilyn awoke, confused and a little angry. Eirene did a remarkable job of deflecting her concerns and explaining about the disaster that befell the corporation. When Marilyn learned how staff had risked their lives to free her from the collapsing building, her concerns evaporated. Eirene led her outside, and her cries of dismay at seeing the inferno echoed through the small building.

Hidden behind the screening sheet, Sarah hugged herself and ran hands along her flanks and limbs, relishing the feeling of being once again herself. She felt only a momentary stab of guilt at deceiving Marilyn, but it passed quickly. The woman wanted to return to youth, and she was getting her chance. The body she wore was very similar to Sarah's, so she'd have nothing to ever complain about.

After a moment, she looked up to find Eirene watching her with a serious expression on her face. The other woman said a little wistfully, "You cannot understand how important your own flesh and bones are until you lose them."

Sarah suddenly had a thought. "Where's your body?"

Eirene gave her a little smile, "It was lost long before Maerwynn got the best of me. Enjoy the time you have, my dear. It's never long enough."

Sarah was not sure what to say to that. Eirene shook off her melancholy and led Sarah to the door. "Try to stay focused. We have much to do."

She explained that Jill and Tomas would spread the word that one of the transfer machines had survived the blast. They would claim it had been in storage, right in the building where the two of them stood. All renters were to be restored immediately.

"There are going to be so many questions," Sarah breathed.

"That's why we have to move fast."

Eirene opened the door, and Sarah was surprised to find Almeda and Tereza, a mousy little woman who was Dr. Maerwynn's final assistant, standing nervously in the doorway. Two burly security officers flanked them.

"Go help Jill," Eirene commanded Sarah, and then motioned the other two women inside.

Outside chaos still reigned. More fire trucks had arrived, along with several news helicopters. It

looked like dozens of police cars had responded to
the disaster, and uniformed officers were trying to
gain control of the bedlam.

Mr. Fleischer's booming voice drew Sarah to
the area where the rows of life support encased bodies lay on gurneys. Staffers formed a barrier between
those bodies and the crowds of desperate renters.

Between the two groups, flanked by his security staff and a dozen police officers, Mr. Fleischer
was calling for calm. Since Sarah had last seen him,
his head had been wrapped with bandages that concealed half his face.

It was not until he turned that Sarah realized
the truth.

Tomas.

Eirene must have swapped his face for Mr.
Fleischer's moments earlier in the ambulance. Probably Mr. Fleischer had been drugged and concealed
while Tomas assumed his identity. Tomas looked
enough like Mr. Fleischer that no one would notice, not with the bandages, and with the panic and
chaos engulfing the ruins of Alterego.

Tomas acquired a bullhorn and used it to restore a semblance of order. Some of the worried
renters looked relieved to learn it would be possible
to return to their own bodies, and lined up eagerly
for the transfer.

Police and medical personnel tried in vain to be allowed in the operating room, but Tomas refused to allow it. He claimed that under the circumstances Alterego's primary objective was the safety of their people.

A staffer appeared at Tomas' side to inform him the makeshift operating room was ready. Sarah and Jill, assisted by some of the other staffers, tried to figure out how to order the transfers. The challenge proved daunting.

Some of the renters' bodies had already been returned to their suites prior to the implosion of the complex, and no one pretended they would find any survivors in the destroyed corporate facility. That left some renters without a body to return to.

At the same time, there were dozens of convict bodies available, either being worn by staffers, or on stretchers as spares, that would never be reincorporated since the souls of those convicts had been destroyed in the vault.

Questions of identity and ownership sparked dozens of arguments, threats of legal action, and three separate fist-fights. Tomas, acting as Mr. Fleischer, made several executive orders to push the process forward.

Pitched as a temporary solution, he ordered renters to be returned to their bodies whenever possible.

If their bodies were suspected destroyed in the fire, they were to transfer to available convict bodies so the donors could also be restored.

"That's not good enough," shouted one red-faced elderly gentleman who tried vainly to push his walker closer through the crowd. "You're guilty of criminal negligence, if not outright manslaughter. I refuse to trust you or your company after what you did to my wife."

His wife, a woman wearing 'Southern Belle,' who hovered close beside him, crossed her arms defiantly and added, "You killed my body, so I'm not transferring anywhere."

Several other donors echoed those cries, and Sarah began to worry. Renters under normal circumstances were often reluctant to return to their old, decrepit bodies. Despite the shock of the disaster, they had a perfect opportunity to try to hold onto the youth they spent so much money renting. Led by 'Southern Belle,' a large percentage of them appeared ready to fight to do so.

Tomas responded without hesitation. Gesturing at his heavily bandaged face, he cried, "Guilty you say? I am guilty! Guilty of caring too much for all of you!"

Despite a chorus of angry words, he added, "As soon as I learned of the potential risks this week,

I've worked day and night to learn the truth. Only hours ago, I finally gained access to Dr. Maerwynn's secret files and discovered that she's been lying to us all. She and one of her assistants, a deceitful woman named Mai Luan, deceived Alterego and buried evidence of the health risks."

"I confronted them today, and when they learned I planned to reveal the truth, despite the risks to my company, they attacked me and set off the chain reaction that destroyed this complex." As he spoke, an actual tear glistened in his one visible eye.

The crowd's angry muttering faded away under his masterful performance. He added more quietly, "I barely escaped that firetrap with my life, thanks to the bravery of some of my staff."

Pointing to the angry old gentleman, Tomas added, "So save your anger for those who perpetrated this crime."

The old fellow frowned, "You're the president. You're responsible."

"Yes I am," Tomas added loudly. "I take full responsibility for the safety of my people, and for your safety. But the legal wrangling and finger pointing can wait." To the stubborn woman wearing 'Southern Belle' he added, "First, we need to save your life."

The woman gasped, as did many others. "What do you mean?"

Tomas paused to ensure he had everyone's attention. "I learned today that the reason rental time limits were capped at three months was to avoid serious psychological risks. Dr. Maerwynn's secret experiments had confirmed that without a costly new set of safety protocols, people living in other bodies faced a ninety-nine percent chance of catastrophic mental collapse, resulting in a permanent vegetative state or death."

Sarah wished she could speak with Tomas privately. She doubted those risks were true, but he spoke with such passion she could not be sure.

Even as a new wave of panic rippled through the crowd, he held up his hands and spoke over them. "Thankfully, a single transfer unit, our most recent prototype, installed with those vital safety protocols, has survived the catastrophe. My staff has already prepared a functional operating room to enable return to your original bodies, or transfer to temporary replacements safe from those long-term risks."

Renters began clamoring for immediate transfer, and the previously obstinate woman wearing 'Southern Belle' was one of the loudest.

They worked straight through until almost midnight before the last transfer was complete, while police and medical examiners waited impatiently to interrogate Almeda and Tereza. As Dr. Maerwynn's only available assistants who understood the full process, they were people of interest in the investigation.

After the last patient was released and the security officer manning the door allowed them to enter, officials swarmed into the building.

Sarah had been resting on a nearby folding chair, enjoying the blissful feeling of being herself. But she sat forward to listen as cries of alarm rang from the building and more police raced to respond. White-coated doctors pushed two gurneys out through the crowd, followed by uniformed officers carrying a pair of opened life support units. On the gurneys lay the bodies of Almeda and Tereza.

Their faces were missing.

So exhausted was Sarah that it took her a moment to understand everyone's excitement. She'd grown numb to the horror of the faceless bodies, to the shock and revulsion that everyone else was experiencing only for the first time.

"I should have expected this."

Eirene seated herself in a nearby chair, her expression sour. "I thought I had them contained, that I'd have time to interrogate them once the transfers completed, but I underestimated their resourcefulness."

"How'd they escape?"

Eirene considered the question a moment before responding. "Most likely they double stacked like I did with Jill. If I'd been paying proper attention, I might have realized what they were doing."

"What did you want to ask them about?"

Eirene gave her a surprised look. "Haven't you been paying attention, my dear? I need to know about that machine they developed, and why they were harvesting souls in the vault. How long have they been working with the cui dashi and . . . well, many other things."

"But Mai Luan is dead."

Eirene chuckled and patted Sarah's knee. "Your optimism is so refreshing."

"But she blew up a building around herself." Sarah gestured at the still-smoldering ruins.

"With so many souls to draw upon, there was no way Mai Luan committed suicide. No, she escaped somehow and destroyed the building behind her to conceal the evidence."

"How is that possible?"

Fresh shouting interrupted Eirene. Angry voices rose in volume from the small building where the transfers had been taking place.

"No doubt they finally overcame their shock at finding those bodies," Eirene observed. "They're realizing there is no transfer machine in the building."

Sarah said, "I feel sorry for them. They're trying to investigate things they can't hope to understand."

"No, they cannot. I'm the one who has to get to the bottom of this."

"How?"

"I'll start with the last people they transferred. That may produce some leads."

Eirene rose just as Jill arrived and flopped down into a nearby chair.

"Wait, I have so many questions still," Sarah said.

"Another time, I'm afraid." Eirene shook her hand solemnly. "It was a pleasure, Sarah. You did well in there."

"We'd have been lost without you."

Jill snorted. "What world have you been living in, Sarah? Psycho lady's not our friend."

"You have no idea," Sarah said.

With a final wave, Eirene slipped away into the crowd.

Jill frowned at her back. "We should sick the cops on her."

"Don't you dare. She saved our lives."

Jill waved a hand across the devastated landscape. "Sarah, our lives are a mess. Look around."

How could she explain that despite the chaos surrounding them, she finally felt her life was back where it needed to be? Instead she rose and gave Jill a little hug. "Thanks for your help today."

"I'm just glad we didn't go nuts." Jill sighed. "What are we going to do next?"

Sarah nodded toward the swarms of media personnel. "Like they say, when one door closes . . ."

Jill barked a laugh and finished for her. "Don't get your fingers caught."

Together they moved toward the news cameras.

Within minutes, every camera was focused on Jill, who gave a masterful performance expressing condolences to staff, donors and renters alike who suffered from the tragedy.

As reporters peppered Jill with questions and she warmed to the attention, Sarah slipped back into the crowd. Jill was going to be all right.

CHAPTER 29

Dressed in tan, cotton slacks and a white blouse, Marilyn rang the doorbell at Walter and Gladys' house. A maid answered the door and showed her to the back patio.

Instead of sunning their gorgeous bodies in skimpy swimsuits like the last time she had seen them, the couple sat in padded chairs under a wide awning near the pool. Gladys was arguing with her nurse about some medication, while Walter sat hunched in front of a small table piled high with official looking documents. Two men in suits flanked him, and they were talking heatedly.

When Marilyn arrived, Walter rose to greet her. He looked haggard, with deep circles under his eyes. While Gladys had been restored to her own aging body, his had been destroyed in the fire, so Alterego had provided him the body of a convict. It looked young and fit and the tattoos were easily covered by his shirt.

Seeing the two of them together drove home the tragedy for Marilyn. Despite claims by Alterego that they would set everything right, they could never restore Walter to his former self. He was stuck in a different generation than his wife, and would be doomed to watch her die in a few years while he would live for decades.

As the horror of it settled over her, she fought to hide a wave of tears by giving Walter a fierce hug. Then she knelt beside Gladys and gently embraced her.

"How are you?"

Gladys managed a weak smile, but Walter growled, "We're in a right mess, Marilyn. Look at us."

"Is there any hope?" she couldn't help but ask.

"I don't see any." He dropped back into his chair. "I mean, I'm sure I could find some old guy willing to swap with me, but the technology was lost. No one knows how to do it any more."

"They'll think of something, dear," Gladys said with forced confidence.

"I hope so. In the meantime, it's a legal fiasco."

"Have you heard any more news from the congressional hearings?" Marilyn asked. Although her contract had been lost in the fire, no one had yet contested her ownership of the young body she wore. Walter was not so lucky.

He waved at the piles of legal documents on the table. "We're mired in a mess that'll take years to clear up, and threatens to consume all our life savings. In the meantime, there are hundreds of lawsuits out there. There's no precedent for this, and no one even has the final count of the dead. All the records were lost."

"I heard the family is suing you."

"Just one of the suits they filed. They filed for wrongful death of Jim, the guy whose body I ended up with, but life insurance companies don't know how to react. Do they count him as dead, or me? His consciousness is gone, but his body is living. My body is dead, but I'm still here."

Gladys piped in, "According to the courts, they're still trying to decide who poor Walter is."

"And if they decide I'm really Jim, then his family is preparing to sue me for child support!"

Marilyn didn't know how to respond. She hadn't considered all the legal issues hovering just under the surface of the rental program. She'd only ever focused on the fantastic gift of being young again.

"At least you have clear legal ownership," Gladys said to try to steer the conversation to a happier topic.

"Yes," she nodded, but couldn't help adding with a sniffle, "But when Bill learned the truth, he left me."

"Oh dear, you poor thing," Gladys said, and opened her arms for Marilyn to come for another hug.

"He doesn't deserve you then," Walter said harshly. "You'll find a better one, don't worry. Any man in his right mind would want you."

Gladys whispered into Marilyn's ear, "After I'm gone . . ."

Marilyn recoiled, shocked by the implied suggestion.

Gladys gave her a sad smile and whispered, "Don't be such an old lady, Marilyn. You're the only person I know that I'd feel comfortable for Walter to marry after I'm gone."

Walter pretended not to hear, and the conversation turned to mundane gossip. Marilyn excused herself a few minutes later when the nurse reminded Gladys it was time for her afternoon nap.

As she slipped behind the wheel of her Cadillac, she wondered at the marvelous gift of youth she'd purchased. Was it a gift, or a curse?

CHAPTER 30

T omas slipped into the chair opposite Sarah in a small Italian restaurant. "Hi. Sorry I'm late."

"You look good," Sarah said with a smile. "Must've lost what, fifty pounds?"

Tomas grimaced. "More like a hundred. It's good to be home."

"I saw you on television. Great performance."

"I'm just glad it's over."

"You pulled it off. Alterego is gone."

In the last week, Tomas had overseen Alterego's dissolution, still disguised as Mr. Fleischer. Most of the blame for the disaster had been directed toward Dr. Maerwynn and Mai Luan. At first the two of them were presumed dead, but Tomas had leaked the rumor that at least one of them may have escaped the facility before it blew. A massive manhunt had begun for them, along with the other two missing assistants.

With the technology lost, along with all the company's documents, the health risks that had precipitated the panic remained unconfirmed rumors. Tomas had ensured that all the senior staff were fired without severance pay, and had routed most of the company's remaining capital into bonuses for donors and to the legal defense fund. Sarah and Jill, named two of the brave staffers who had helped save Mr. Fleischer's life, had walked away with ridiculously huge payouts.

Lawsuits had multiplied like wildfire in high summer. Courts all across the country struggled with questions of legal identity, and many legislatures argued about passing bills to help clarify things. As usual, their ideas varied so wildly they would likely just complicate the situation.

Religious groups had come out condemning everyone involved as spawn of Satan, while other groups had seized upon the use of convict bodies. They proposed that the technology be adopted to swap convicted felons with good, upstanding elderly people. That way, felons convicted of life sentences would die sooner, freeing up much-needed taxpayer funds, while the elderly who received their bodies would get a well-deserved extension on life.

All of those ideas were little more than speculation, though, since no one knew how to replicate the supposed technology.

After taking a long drink Tomas said, "Mr. Fleischer woke up today to a legal firestorm."

"He deserves it."

"Agreed. I just wish Almeda and Tereza hadn't slipped away."

"Is Eirene still hunting them?"

"Undoubtedly. But she's got other priorities too."

"Like what?"

Tomas smiled. "We'll talk about it later. What about you? What are your plans?"

Sarah raised her glass. "Well, since I'm flush with cash for life, I have lots of options."

"You going to start dating high profile suitors like Jill?"

Sarah laughed, but shook her head.

"You're number five. You could be a celebrity."

Jill had chosen that road and was quickly becoming the hottest name in the media, with many very wealthy suitors jockeying for her attention.

"So what are you thinking?" Tomas asked gently.

"Not sure. What about you?"

Tomas grinned. "I'm taking a vacation."

Sarah laughed.

"Want to join me?"

Sarah hesitated, considering Tomas. He was the most interesting man she'd ever met. She owed him her life. More than her life. But he was more than what he pretended to be.

The question of what Tomas was, of who he was, intrigued her. She felt sure he was a good man, perhaps a man she did want to pursue getting to know more intimately.

Just as importantly, he knew Eirene, and understood the freaky world of magic and souls and face masks. Sarah felt drawn to that world, felt an intense desire to understand what Mai Luan was doing and what those runes meant.

Tomas could explain it. He could bring her to Eirene, guide her into their secret world, warn her of the dangers lurking in the shadows. Sarah needed to speak with Eirene, and wanted to understand what she'd witnessed.

One of the most important things driving her to understand was the chaos still enshrouding so many innocent lives. Eirene alone might be able to help restore those lives wrecked by Alterego.

So when Tomas raised his glass, Sarah clinked hers to it and made up her mind.

She smiled. "I just might do that."

know, that ended way too soon. What happens next?

Lots.

Sarah has only one regret.

Nope, it's not toppling a billion-dollar body renting industry. They had it coming.

It's the other victims who didn't get their bodies back.

Sarah wants answers, and Tomas has them. So his cryptic invitation to visit New Orleans actually sounds fun.

Until people start trying to kill her.

The centuries-long war between the facetakers and their rune-enhanced enemies escalates dramatically, and the fight plunges back into history.

Not what she would call a great first date. Especially when they land in WWII Berlin and a psycho near-immortal wants Sarah's soul on a platter.

If you loved *Saving Face*, you need to read *Memory Hunter*. It's an action-packed thrill ride, full of history and cool magic. And you can get it at https://smarturl.it/sp55pq

Congratulations! You've joined the growing community who have read and loved *Saving Face*.

I know you're eager to dive right into *Memory Hunter*, but want to learn more about Eirene's husband, Gregorios, first?

You've unlocked access to some super cool exclusive content. It's a short story called "Face Lift." It takes place at the same time as *Saving Face*. Consider it a secret thank you to my best readers. Here's a brief description of "Face Lift":

Gregorios infiltrates an island medical retreat, hunting for his lost wife. He suspects the facility conceals a dark secret, but what he finds dwarfs his worst fears.

This thrilling story pits resourceful Gregorios against deadly adversaries that somehow connect with the sinister plan Mai Luan was hatching in the vault under Alterego.

Get your copy of "Face Lift" using this link: https://dl.bookfunnel.com/kxaracrlhy.

To make the download process as easy as possible, I use BookFunnel, the best site for downloading book content safely and easily. You'll need to provide your email address for BookFunnel to send you the story. (You will not get added to any lists. If you want to join my newsletter, there's a link on the next page.)

AUTHOR'S NOTE

S *aving Face* came about more by accident than any grand plan. The idea of facetakers came to me in a freaky dream several years ago. It was one of those super-vivid dreams that lingered long after waking and sent shivers down my spine as I related it to my wife.

Haunted by the concept, I wrote my first-ever short story, titled "Face Lift," which ended up winning honorable mention in the 2010 Writers of the Future contest. That's the exclusive content I just offered you. I highly recommend it.

I hope you enjoy the rest of the series as much as I do!

Frank